Finalist for the
GABRIEL GARCÍA MÁRQUEZ SHORT STORY PRIZE
2018

Shortlisted for the
SOCIETY OF AUTHORS TA FIRST TRANSLATION PRIZE
2019

'Fuentes is a consistently engaging and original writer (…). It is a joy to find writing of such high quality'
TIMES LITERARY SUPPLEMENT

'The collection successfully blends sharp dialogue, striking images, and consequential action. These satisfying stories are full of surprises.'
PUBLISHERS WEEKLY

'Fuentes's unflinching eye for the horror of small-scale conflict is hypnotic.'
THE QUIETUS

'Quirky, dynamic and thoughtful'
THE SKINNY

'The collection masterfully toys with the conventions of its genre.'
REVIEW31

'A startling take on what it means to be human. (…) A quiet gem.'
THE MONTHLY BOOKING

TROUT, BELLY UP

First published by Charco Press 2019

Charco Press Ltd., Office 59, 44-46 Morningside Road, Edinburgh EH10 4BF
Copyright © 2017 Rodrigo Fuentes

First published in Spanish as *Trucha panza arriba*
English translation copyright © Ellen Jones 2019

A CIP catalogue record for this book is available from
the British Library.

ISBN: 9781916465619
e-book: 9781916465688

www.charcopress.com

Edited by Fionn Petch
Cover design by Pablo Font
Typeset by Sam R. Johnson
Proofread by Fiona Mackintosh
Printed by TJ Books Limited

2 4 6 8 10 9 7 5 3

Supported using public funding by
**ARTS COUNCIL
ENGLAND**

Rodrigo Fuentes

TROUT, BELLY UP

Translated by
Ellen Jones

CHARCO PRESS

CHARCO PRESS

TROUT, BELLY UP

That family stuff's complicated, I told Don Henrik. He'd just asked about Ermiña, who'd been my cousin, then my girlfriend, and is now my wife. The thing is, I told him, it's hard to find a woman like Ermiña up here in the mountains. She keeps the kids in line and makes a finger-licking-good chicken soup, but she also knows when to pick a fight and when not to. When's that then? asked Don Henrik. Well, if I don't get my coffee in the morning, she knows it's not worth it. Any other time, sure. But no coffee, then a whole day out on the trout farm – how can she possibly pick a fight with me after that? What I didn't tell him is the way Ermiña curls up to me on cold nights, or how she looked all those years ago when I glimpsed her bathing in the river, her plump body shiny with soap. She wasn't surprised to see me coming out of the bushes, clumsily taking off my clothes, and she just stood there, a look of amusement on her face as I stumbled over the rocks on the riverbank.

We only had girls, Ermiña and me, I told Don Henrik, not a single boy. I tried to focus on my feet, squeezed into the rubber boots Don Henrik himself had given me. First came Tatinca, I said, then Ileana. The third was Ilopanga, and the last one we called José, for Maria José. We tried to get José into football. The other three would stay at home with their mum while José and I took the ball up the mountain. I'd pass it and José would knock it back to me, and so we went through the back of beyond, tiki-taka to and fro, until one of my passes went too high and José bravely went in for a header but instead stopped the ball dead with her nose. So that was our last training session. Since then the kid's barely left Ermiña's side, I told Don Henrik. A proper limpet, poor love.

Don Henrik took a drag on his little cigarette – all cigarettes look little in his enormous hands – and, looking out at the grove of trees in front of his farm, said that there were worse things in life. And with that we settled the matter, or at least that's what I understood Don Henrik to have decided. He poured more rum into my plastic cup (the glass tumbler was for his use only) and there we sat, on the wooden terrace Juancho and I had built for him.

The syrupy spirit took me back to when I first met Don Henrik, and those long hours I spent in the hammock at my aunt's – Ermiña's mum – wondering what to do about the family expenses, where I was going to find work, or, frankly, how to get the hell out of there. The sheet metal roof reflected different colours depending on what angle you looked at it, and I used to spend whole afternoons craning my neck, trying to find just the shade I was looking for. One day Bartolo came down the lane shouting, in that grating, twangy voice of his, that there was to be a meeting. Hoping to get rid of him, I yelled that I'd be up in a minute, before settling back into the hammock. That was my first mistake: Ermiña, who'd been cooking in the other room, came out to see what was going on. The two of them spoke quietly outside, and before long I felt her approach (it freaks me out how silent she can be sometimes), stick her face over the side of the hammock, and ask me to please go with Bartolo. She stood there unmoving until I got up.

In the community centre, which still doesn't have a roof, Don Henrik had stacked two plastic chairs one on top of the other (the only way they'd hold his weight). Sitting facing him were Tito Colmenares, Bartolo, and Juancho. Juancho scowled at me as soon as I came in. We're cousins too and I think that's why he resents me. Ermiña once hinted that Juancho thought I was a good-for-nothing, and we've been sizing each other up from a distance, silently cursing each other ever since. Ermiña seems less bothered about it now, as though Juancho confirmed her suspicions about him with his spitefulness.

That afternoon Don Henrik talked about his life out east, about the melon plantations he'd set up, about other 'interesting' projects, and my mind had just started to wander when he opened the icebox between his feet and pulled a huge fish out by its tail.

Do you know what this is? he asked, holding it up.

We shifted in our seats, glancing at each other.

It's a trout, said Don Henrik, ignoring someone's raised hand. A rainbow trout.

He turned the creature over, as though wanting the sun to catch all its hidden colours, but in truth it just looked like any old fish.

This right here is going to bring progress to the mountain, he said, and lifted the trout even higher.

That's when I realised Don Henrik was a bit barmy, and I started to warm to him.

Don Henrik had travelled all over the world, and in Norway, he told us that afternoon, he'd learned all there was to know about breeding trout. Gesturing towards the top of the mountain and his plot of land, he described where the first cement tanks would go – three metres in diameter, eight hundred trout in each one – and detailed how he'd filter the water, connect pipes up to the spring, feed and fillet the fish.

3

When he finished he got to his feet, still holding the fish by the tail, and asked us to line up in front of him. We all looked at each other, a bit confused. Fine, said Don Henrik, resigned to the fact that nobody was moving. He stared at me a long while, but I think it was just because I've got a big nose – it always gets people's attention. Then he looked round at the rest of them, one by one, and in the end gestured, trout in hand, to Juancho and Bartolo. Those two were chosen to start work on the trout farm.

If Bartolo hadn't broken his leg the next day when a pregnant cow attacked him in the middle of a field, I'd still be lying in that same hammock at my aunt's place. But fortunes can change, even if no one ever gets any richer.

Work on the trout farm's been hard. The nights are cold up here, and after levelling the ground and building the first two tanks Don Henrik ran out of money. He had to go back to the capital to find more, leaving Juancho and me in charge. At least I've got my family to keep me company. Don Henrik just about manages to scrape together our wages, and visits every couple of weeks to see how the project's progressing, which it never is, though I suppose things aren't getting any worse either.

Ermiña and I have had some problems. I have to admit: it's not all happy families on the trout farm.

★

The first problem is Juancho. Let's just say he's got the same nose as me (although not quite so prominent), drags his feet when he walks – sign of a bad conscience – and sometimes when I talk to him he just stares at me, unblinking, with those cow eyes of his, like he's got no idea what I'm saying. This annoys me, because I know he might be slow but he's not a total imbecile. I could be telling him that one of the fish tanks has got a crack in it or describing the latest Parcelas match, his expression would be exactly the same. I've thought about goading him into a fight, ambushing him down some dark track, but he's bigger and stronger than me and losing to him would be a real blow.

The second problem with Juancho is that he came up here to get away from something. It's obvious, no matter how tight-lipped he is. We've got our routine now: I clean the tanks and take care of feeding and looking after the trout. I also give Ermiña a hand in the vegetable garden next to our hut, where the clearing with the tanks ends and the forest begins. Juancho patrols the plot day and night, doing the necessary repairs and making sure all the pipes are working properly. He likes to take the rifle out with him, the one Don Henrik left us, but he also carries a pistol in his belt. One time I found him in the forest, sitting on the trunk of a fallen oak. He was looking up above the trees where occasionally you'll catch sight of a quetzal, the pistol in his hand. I wouldn't have been surprised to see him fire a bullet into one of those poor birds. Ermiña told me (God knows how she finds these things out) that some men came by his shack to leave him a message, before he moved up here. They asked him for money – too much money. They're relations from down the mountain, Ermiña told me, it's something to do with inheritance. I think that's why he wanted to work with Don Henrik, to get away from that side of the mountain and be closer to the summit, up here where the only access is along a muddy track.

Juancho goes into the forest every day and disappears off towards the spring where the pipes start. He sits there listening to the water bubbling away, or doing who knows what, and then he'll walk around the edge of the plot until he comes out down below, where the waste water from the tanks drains into the river. I've followed him, and let me tell you, that man does not bear his burden lightly. Sometimes, from the tanks, I see his face appear out of the forest and look carefully around him before he emerges. And at night, when we turn out the lights in our hut, I glance down at the metal shack where he sleeps and see his little candle through the darkness. His stubborn silence has started to scare my daughters, and the truth is it's getting to me too. I don't want my family anywhere near a victim of extortion, let alone one that doesn't pay up when he's asked.

★

Trout are delicate creatures and can't handle temperatures over thirteen degrees. That's why Don Henrik bought his land right at the top of the mountain, because he wanted ice cold spring water. But despite being delicate, they're completely savage. They eat meat, even their own. *Little cannibals*, my Ermiña calls them. I remember the first weeks on the trout farm when I'd spend long periods watching them swimming anti-clockwise, all together like a big happy family. One time a trout began to peel off from the group, rising in tighter and tighter circles until it was flapping about near the surface. Its mouth started to gape, and it went belly up, spinning all silvery on its axis. Then something strange happened. Another trout came up to see what was going on, sniffing at its companion, and from one moment to the next the whole tank freaked out. The water was churning, looked like it was boiling, and the surface filled with the metallic flashes of a knife fight. A minute later everything had calmed down. The big family was once again swimming anti-clockwise. There was no sign of the trout that went belly up.

★

I first met Analí when I went down to the village shop one day with José, just after I started work on the trout farm. She placed the bag of cement and the wire on the counter, and, after handing me my change, smiled at my daughter.

So handsome, she said, he looks just like his Dad.

I didn't have the heart to tell her she was a girl. And I know I shouldn't have cared, but I was pleased with the compliment.

The next day I went down again without José. My heart was thumping as I approached the shop, and I hid behind a tree to check whether Analí was with anyone. She looked beautiful in her little dress behind the counter, smiling at something on her phone.

I went in acting all casual and before long was showing her the funny videos I'd saved: a Velorio skit, that clip of a drunk who won't let go of his sippy cup, another of a Chinese peasant riding a huge pig like it's a stallion. Such a pretty laugh, Analí, so quick to make my heart beat faster.

Up here on the trout farm you can hear birds screaming and howler monkeys roaring from the top of the mountain range. My dog Baloo, who guards the farm at night, gets into a scrap with a paca about every three days. He even brought me a coral snake hanging from his muzzle one afternoon.

So we're not exactly alone, though it definitely feels that way. That's why I told Erminã that she and the girls should walk the four kilometres down to the village that weekend, to spend a night with her mum. I'd stay here and look after things with Juancho; if Don Henrik found out I'd taken off, I'd be out of work. As they turned to say goodbye, I melted at the sight of José waving those little hands that one day could be the hands of a great goalie.

I spent a couple of hours tending to the trout, watching the sky turn orange, and when it was almost dark I started heading down myself. Instead of following them to the village, I took the path that skirted the sweetgum plantation, a kilometre from the trout farm. I had to wait half an hour before I spotted the light of a mobile phone in the darkness. It was Analí on her way up to the place we'd agreed on, and I knew she'd seen me because the light started to approach more slowly.

Hello, troublemaker. I was about to give up on you.

What, and leave me here all by myself? she asked.

It was so dark all I could see was her phone screen, the silhouette of her hand barely visible.

As if I could I leave you here alone, I replied.

The heat I'd been carrying around inside me made my whole body tingle.

Analí wheezed as she suppressed a laugh, and I suddenly remembered the noises José used to make, years ago, when she had bad lungs. I shook my head to shake away the thought.

Do you have a boyfriend? I asked her.

Analí took her time answering.

Not anymore, she said after a while.

Lucky me then.

She didn't reply, but I sensed that something had changed in the darkness.

Aren't I? Lucky? I insisted.

Depends, said Analí, on how you see it.

Well from where I'm standing I can't see a thing, I told her.

Me neither, actually, she said.

Her voice was different too.

I felt my way over to her, working out where her body was. And so, in the dark, we began to kiss. God, she was a good kisser.

★

In order to level the ground for the trout farm, Don Henrik had to use a machine brought in from San Agustín. All this was virgin forest, and the machine ploughed night and day through the undergrowth, shifting big rocks half-buried in the ground. He only cut down one caoba, because the trees here are huge and, rightly or wrongly, Don Henrik respects age. That clearing now contains the two tanks, my hut, Juancho's little shack, and the wooden terrace Don Henrik asked us to build, all surrounded by thick forest. You still have to cut it back every day, because every day the ferns, vines and climbers try to gain back territory from us. But I like using the machete to protect this clearing of ours.

The best time of day is evening, when we get together around the tanks. Ermiña comes out of the hut, the girls start appearing from the forest, accompanied by Baloo, and I go and get the bag of fish food. Everyone grabs a handful. We take it over to the edge of the tank, count to three, and at the same time each toss our handful towards the sky. As soon as it touches down the surface is whipped up by the splashing trout. I love watching my girls then, their mouths half open and their eyes wide, as though seeing it all for the first time. Ermiña smiles to herself quietly, focused on our daughters too, and at that moment I'm filled with the kind of happiness I only usually feel when I'm alone on the rock at the top of the mountain. We wait until the splashing dies down, the last smack of a fishtail glinting in the evening light, and then we all go into the hut for dinner.

★

Don Henrik arrived at the trout farm two weeks after my first encounter with Analí. Juancho, my wife and I got together on his terrace and sat on the plastic chairs he'd brought with him on the previous trip. He paid the wages he owed us and asked me to bring him the glass (I've got it in the hut for safekeeping). From the front seat of his 4x4 he brought out three plastic cups and a bottle of rum, and filled them all to the brim.

We've started to make a bit of money, he told us, raising his glass.

We raised ours too and toasted him. Juancho, the faker, made as if the drink was burning his throat. Ermiña took one sip of hers and began to sneeze.

Hallelujah! said Don Henrik, who'd been drinking on his way there, and filled our cups again.

We have new clients, he said, now settled in his chair, two more restaurants in the capital want our trout. This is going to be a huge project, he added, and the glint in his eye as he looked around him began to fire my enthusiasm.

He lit a cigarette and put on his boss's voice to announce that he'd brought a new batch of trout eggs.

Don Henrik orders the eggs from Norway, where he has contacts. When they arrive we have to put them in the incubator, which is really just an ice box, and when they begin to hatch we move them to the first tank to fatten them up.

Rainbow trout eggs are orange with little black dots – those are the baby trout. Don Henrik says in Russia they eat it as caviar, but I can't stand it, personally. With every batch of eggs we learn something new. These days we only have a seven percent mortality rate. I know this for a fact because it's my job to keep the official count, though in reality only six percent of the trout actually die. The remaining one percent I take out of the tanks when they're fat enough and we eat them ourselves. It's the only meal Juancho will share with us. José starts jumping up and down when she sees me piling up logs to one side of the clearing. As soon as the fish have been skewered, the four girls start dancing round the fire. Seeing them like that, happy and wild, makes me jump up and down on the inside myself.

That night Don Henrik got more drunk than usual. We made him up a corner of the hut, shifting the freezer where we keep the trout when they're ready for delivery, and while he was undressing – his huge belly hanging over his white underpants – he repeated again that we were nearly there, that the business was about to take off. At dawn he headed to the capital and didn't come back for a month and a half.

A couple of nights later I was woken by my phone vibrating. The hut lit up with a bluish light and I had to cover the screen with my hand. For a second I thought Erminã had also woken up, but I checked and it turned out just to be her left eye, which sometimes opens when she's asleep. I looked at the message and recognised Analí's number – I knew it off by heart.

Mmmmm, it said.

I went hot all over and my toes started to twitch of their own accord. I turned the phone face down and lay there on my back for a moment, unable to go back to sleep. Mmmmm, I thought, and, unable to control myself, groped around for the phone so I could look at it again.

Mmmmm.

I was on the point of turning it off when I heard a noise in the corner of the room, where the four girls sleep on the mattress Don Henrik gave us when we started the project. I thought I could make out José watching me. Slightly uneasy, I turned off the phone and tried to go back to sleep. I could barely keep my eyes shut.

The next weekend I told Erminã I'd have to take the trout to the bus station in San Agustín. From there we send them to the capital. I got the ice box ready, loading it onto the quad bike Don Henrik had brought for transporting materials. I sent one last message to Analí, agreeing a meeting place, and set off down the hill.

She was waiting for me where the path forked, heading up to the top of the mountain in one direction and down to San Agustín in the other.

Hello troublemaker, I said.

She got on the bike behind me without saying a word.

What did you tell your family? I asked. The smell of Pert Plus was overwhelming. I felt high just from breathing it.

That I was going out with you, that you wanted to *do things* with me.

A warm shiver ran up the back of my neck.

Seriously? I asked.

Seriously. Didn't you tell yours the same? she asked.

And with that we settled the matter. She put her hands around my waist and rested her head on my back.

I had to kick the starter a couple of times. As I was getting the engine going I realised I was going to have to be careful.

We dropped the trout off at the station in San Agustín then headed towards El Templo, a guesthouse run by my pal Maynor. Maynor had put vases of gardenias in the room and two little chocolates rested on the crisp pillow. It was in that room that I realised I was getting rusty, or rather that, frankly, Analí had more experience than I'd imagined, and I'd imagined plenty.

You need to watch it, I told myself again when we emerged from the room an hour later, but promptly forgot. I'd showered to get rid of the smell, although the fragrance of Pert Plus had already made its way inside me, into my blood.

On the way back up Analí held my waist more tightly. When we arrived at the fork in the road she got out without a word, gave me a kiss, and disappeared down the path.

★

When I got back to the trout farm everything was dark. I parked the quad bike to one side of the tanks and turned off the engine. I was heading towards the hut, the water in the tanks murmuring amongst the sounds of the forest, when I saw a silhouette step into the path. My heart skipped a beat.

Juancho was waiting for me, one hand resting on the concrete edge of the tank, the other folded across his body, grasping the strap of the rifle hanging over his shoulder.

Did I scare you? he asked.

Hardly. Did I scare *you*? I responded, with more bravura than logic.

I was just passing, he said.

Right.

It's late, he said.

Yes, I replied.

And you're still up.

I am.

I wanted to make sure… he added, but then seemed to have second thoughts about completing the sentence.

At that moment the clouds parted and for a second the clearing was lit up from above. I realised he was smiling.

I'm going to bed, Juancho.

Of course, he said, you must be tired.

His face gave nothing away as he said this.

We've got a lot of work to do, I said, and, sighing deeply as though burdened by other things, headed up to the hut.

Be careful, he said to my back, and if I didn't slam the door it was only because I didn't want to wake my family. I listened to his footsteps, lighter than usual, heading towards the forest.

★

In the morning my daughters went down to the village to check if their drunk of a schoolteacher had turned up that day. Meanwhile Ermiña was planting some watercress in the vegetable garden and I went to look for Juancho in the forest.

I found him up by the deep spring, standing motionless looking at the water. I stayed out of sight for a while behind a couple of big swiss cheese plants, thinking how easy it would be to give him a little shove. I stood there as long as five minutes, delighted by the idea, but then Juancho suddenly spoke, as if he had eyes in the back of his head.

You enjoying the shade back there?

I emerged from the greenery and stood beside him. There was something mesmerising about the deep spring water.

I wanted to talk to you, I said.

I figured as much, he responded, and then added: Can't be easy, your situation.

Actually, it was *your* situation I wanted to talk about. It must be tough having them after you like this.

He wrinkled his nose and I realised I'd caught him off guard

They've been asking about you in San Agustín.

Oh yeah?

His voice was a ghost of what it had been earlier.

'Fraid so, I told him.

Who was asking?

There were two of them, I told him. They spoke to me.

I saw him swallow.

And what did they want?

Not much, just asking after you, how you've been.

And what did you tell them?

I crouched by the edge of the spring and put my hand in the water. It really was freezing.

I asked them who they were.

Right, he said. And?

They said they were friends of yours.

Anything else?

Well, I had a bad feeling about them.

So...

So. I told them I didn't know, that it was ages since I'd seen you.

Juancho slowly let his lungs empty.

Right, he said. That's good.

You'll know better than me, I told him. But...

But what?

Well, what I said before, that's all. I had a bad feeling about them.

Juancho moved his head from side to side like he was trying to reconcile two conflicting thoughts, but before he could say anything I turned tail and headed back to the tanks.

All that night I remained wakeful, despite my modest triumph. I had to get up a few times and stand by the tanks, letting the sound of the water soothe me. From there I could see Juancho pass by every now and again as he did the rounds, watching over the farm and making sure the water was still flowing through the pipes to the tanks.

He walked with his head lowered, as though a great weight was bearing down on the nape of his neck, and I felt a little bit sorry, but a lot more cheerful.

*

At one point, not long after the project started, the trout started dying. Every morning I'd wake up and find three or four little bodies floating on the surface of the tank. The rest were drifting around dopily – they wouldn't even eat the dying ones. Don Henrik had to come up from the capital and spend a week here, sleeping in San Agustín every night only to come back up early the next morning. He spent long periods watching the trout, thoughtful, one finger on his lips.

They're suffocating, he said on the fifth day.

As well as a specific temperature, trout need a lot of oxygen. In tanks they get through it quickly with all their swimming. That's how they breathe, but it also tires them out. Fresh water needs to be coming in all the time, oxygenating the tank, and with so many trout there wasn't enough. What's the point in being modest? It was me who figured out how to solve the oxygen problem. I created a *Venturi effect*, according to Don Henrik, who knows about these things. All I did was fiddle about with some plastic tubes, inserting them halfway into the water to create vacuums. I managed to get them to suck air in from outside and bubble it through the water, and that way, from then on, we made sure they had enough oxygen.

You're an empirical engineer, Don Henrik told me after my success. An engineer through and through.

Don Henrik's compliments are almost as flattering as Analí's.

*

But I was troubled to note that at night Ermiña too was tossing and turning in bed. Something was going on with her. On a trip down to the shop for pesticide for the vegetable garden, I took the opportunity to have a quiet word with Analí.

It's better if we don't see each other here anymore.

It's nicer up at the fork in the road, or somewhere else, don't you think?

Why? she asked.

What do you mean why?

Why?

I waited, motionless, my thumbs in my belt, looking at her without understanding. But Analí let out a laugh and started looking at her phone. I just stood there in front of the counter like an idiot. Some men came in to buy something and all there was left to do was go. She didn't even say goodbye.

I sent her a couple of texts in the days that followed, but she didn't reply. That week I completely lost it. At certain moments I felt an enormous relief, like suddenly I could breathe, and I was overcome with affection for Ermiña and my girls, swiftly followed by a horrible guilt. A minute later I'd be tearing my hair out with the sheer desire to see Analí. It was time to harvest the trout and the rains were getting heavier. I worked hard through the downpour, pulling out one fish after another, trying to drive away my desire. But that only made me think about her more, my own sweat reminding me of our nights together, and then I'd be hit by the smell of Pert Plus, followed by that scent behind her ears, just like a baby's, and that in turn reminded me of her breath, her sweet-sour breath, discovering all her perfumes as though for the first time. But memories of smells disappear as quickly as they come, and it hit me how great a distance there was between my body and hers, and that made me so profoundly sad that I had to stop and lean against the edge of the tank.

As though she could hear my actual thoughts, that afternoon I received a message from her.

I want to do things to you in your bed :)

That sentence threw me into a total spin. I read it so

many times that José came over to ask what I was looking at. Erminia didn't say anything, which should have put me on my guard, but in truth I was walking on air, barely able to hide my grin. Which bed was she talking about? The one in the hut? Do things… here? From one moment to the next everything around me was infused with Anali, her laugh tangled in the forest, her breath bubbling with the water, her body pressing insistently against mine. And Erminia was right there, silent, making lunch, working in the vegetable garden, helping the girls with homework she'd devised herself.

My daughters went out earlier than usual the next morning. I was sharpening the machete to cut back the edges of the clearing when Erminia came over. She had a big bag with her and was wearing makeup, which she never does up here.

They told me, she said.

I turned to look at her.

Told you what?

For God's sake, she said. You're pathetic.

Dizziness flooded through me, so much so that I had to crouch down. When I raised my eyes, Erminia was looking down at me. She smiled, just a little, her lips very tight and her eyes sad, and made her way towards the path down the mountain. I thought about following her, saying something, shouting at her or pleading, but she was walking so upright, her skirt cupping her big buttocks so nicely, holding her bag so firmly, that I didn't have the guts. I went cold all over and let myself fall onto my backside. A sharp whistling started up in my ears, and it was a few minutes before I could clear my head and get up again.

Oh fuck, I thought. Fuck fuck fuck.

I felt half-cut for the rest of the day, wandering from the tanks to the hut, from the hut to the edge of the forest, from the forest to the vegetable garden, and in the vegetable garden I stood looking at all the little plants Ermiña had grown in the last few months – chard, tomatoes, tufts of watercress – all so carefully tended. I went and got a bucket of water from the tanks, thinking I'd water any that looked like they needed it, but none of them did, and I noted the care she'd taken over every single plant, the furrows dug so neatly, the topsoil well-turned, and then I just stood there, a long time, until my throat began closing and tears started to fall one after the other from my eyes. I don't know how long I was there, thinking about my daughters, imagining Ermiña picking them up from school and telling them that they weren't going back up the hill that afternoon, they were going all the way down to their grandmother's house. The rain intensified and soaked my hair, my face, my body.

Suddenly I found myself walking down the path that led away from the farm, walking faster and faster, tripping as I raced down, my rubber boots slipping, and with them this body, this body that wasn't mine, a clumsy, borrowed body that was taking me to my wife whether I liked it or not. I managed to slow it down when I got to the village. I felt my way over to a rock we used to call The Bull because of its shape, and sat on the animal's back. Little by little I began to calm down. Going after Ermiña was crazy, no matter how you looked at it, and the idea of seeing my aunt was just plain stupid. Once I'd figured that much out, I began to feel resentful.

They told me, Ermiña had said.

When I realised, rage began to pulse through my body and I knew that Juancho had given me away. This is where it's hard to find the words, because in that moment I hated Juancho, and myself, but also, why not say it, Ermiña too. What had she done? Or not done? I was struggling to put my finger on it, but I was sure there was something crouching there, as present and solid as the stone I was sitting on.

As though possessed by the devil, I jumped down from The Bull and headed back uphill. As I climbed, it finally sank in that Ermiña wouldn't be there, nor Tatinca, nor Ileana, nor Ilopanga, and definitely not José. Distress started to wash away my rage, replacing it with a grim coldness. When I arrived at the entrance to the farm I saw Juancho sitting by his little shack, his rifle hanging over his shoulder. The rain had abated and heavy clouds were rising over the mountainside, by turns hiding and illuminating the clearing, so that sometimes I could see Juancho's hunched figure and sometimes not. As I got closer I had the impression that I was approaching a very tired ghost.

You have to go, I said, now almost level with him.

He turned to look at me, slowly but not surprised.

What?

Go, I told him, now.

Why?

Swallowing saliva, I made an effort to keep my voice calm.

I saw those guys you know, down below. They're on their way up.

Down below?

Not that far, I explained. They'd already reached the village.

They spoke to you?

No, I said, thinking on my feet, they just saw me in the distance and starting talking amongst themselves. I'm telling you, they're heading up here.

His hand reached for the pistol in his belt.

Now?

Now, I told him.

Juancho stood, and then stared intently at the spot where the path reaches the farm. He started looking around him, along the line where the clearing ends and the forest begins.

For sure?

For sure, Juancho, go.

He took out the pistol, loaded it, and ran into his shack. A minute later he was back with his rucksack.

He turned to look around him one more time with his big cow eyes and, without saying goodbye, ran off towards the path down the hill. Halfway there he stopped. He turned on the spot and ran back up, stumbling.

Take this, he said, pulling the rifle over his head as he approached. You might need it.

Why would I need it?

That's how they are, he said. Be careful.

I almost felt alarmed. Seeing him like that, his hair a mess and his jaw clenched, I thought, for a second, about telling him the truth. But José's little hands flashed through my mind again, waving goodbye, and the moment passed.

Go, I told him, go quickly.

He slipped across the farm towards the path, seemed to change his mind, then made for the edge of the clearing and disappeared into the forest.

I went into the hut and looked at the bed Ermiña had made up, the girls' mattress leaning against the wooden boards of the wall so she could clean, the whole room dark and neat. I sat down on the edge of the bed, leant back, and seeing the metal roof suddenly heard my girls laughing outside, chasing the dog Baloo around the tanks. But the noise dissolved into the sound of trickling water, and then I felt like I was sinking into the mattress, as though I could fall right through it. I tried to think of something else, to shake off my longing, and remembered Anali's message. I dug around in my trousers for my phone.

I want to do things to you...

My body responded. *I want to do things to you...* I read it again, maybe even said it out loud. I imagined her topless, naked, on me, just like I'd imagined her a thousand times. Clutching her own little breasts in her hands, lifting her gaze to the ceiling. I typed the message furiously, barely even looking at the screen.

Her reply arrived within a couple of minutes.

I'll meet you above the village at six.

I was late going to get her and ran recklessly down the hill, my insides roiling with emotion. I found her by an enormous oak tree, just where the sweetgum plantation begins to turn into forest. At least my silence matched hers this time. We headed up to the farm.

I'm glad you're alone, she said eventually, when we reached the clearing.

The forest had gone silent, as though the plants, the water, the animals and the birds had all quietened down in their own little corners, attentive to this new presence. Even Baloo had disappeared.

I didn't reply. Her scent hit me and already that was almost too much. But being like that, on the verge of setting everything alight, lost for words, did me good.

I saw her cast an eye over the farm, curious, and above all satisfied. She went over to one of the tanks and dipped a finger in the water.

It's cold, she said, then put her finger in her mouth and sucked it.

That water tastes of fish, I know because I've done the same, but with the way she was looking at me it could have been the sacred fountain of our unbridled passion.

And this is your place? she asked, eyeing the hut.

It had started to rain again, and before I could answer she was already stepping lightly towards the door. She opened it and let herself in. I followed her and lit a candle on the night table. Heavy raindrops started to thunder on the metal roof, gathering strength as Analí explored, walking around the bed to examine the flower design on the quilt, going over to the calendar featuring pictures of Swiss meadows that Don Henrik had put up on the wall, using her toes to toy with the mothballs Ermiña had put down in the corners. Then she turned to me and wrinkled her nose.

It smells... different, here, she said.

I didn't like the way she said it, but she'd already crouched down to pick up a little rubber ball from under the bed.

Is this your daughter's? she asked.

I said yes without knowing which one she meant.

She's so little. I love her smile, she said, and I realised at once that she was talking about José, who's got these white teeth that light the whole place up when she's happy.

Analí sat down on the bed and looked up at me, rolling the little rubber ball between her hands.

You remember her then, I said.

I don't have to remember her, I talk to her every day when she comes out of school.

Right. So – you know each other well then?

She didn't answer, but neither did she look away. She let go of the little ball, which fell and rolled across the floor, and then she put one hand on her thigh.

But do you talk to her a lot? I pressed.

She tilted her head, made a face, and sighed before answering.

Well yeah, she tells me what's going on up here. Your work, the delicious trout. She even told me... Having started, she then seemed to regret it, and let out a little laugh.

What?

She looked down, as though deciding how to go on.

That you barely look at your wife.

She wouldn't say that.

Analí turned over the hand on her thigh, lifting it a little, but after a while it went back to its place.

Well what did you say to her?

Analí gave another half laugh.

That's between me and your daughter.

Her tone took me by surprise, but a growing irritation made me hold her gaze, giving nothing away, or perhaps betraying everything, an idea that shook me even more. I imagined her in the shop with José, the girl's little hands on the edge of the counter as she listened carefully, and then I saw José leave and talk to Ilopanga, sitting outside school with one of her friends, and Ilopanga whispering something to Ileana on the way up to the trout farm, their two faces serious, and then Ileana sitting beside Tatinca on this same bed in the hut, saying something into her ear. The conversation between Tatinca and Ermiña I couldn't, didn't want to imagine. The rain let loose and the sound of it beating on the metal filled the hut and my head.

I hated Analí as she stretched her hand out to me, and I hated myself as I took it. All this turned me on even more. She pulled me gently closer and made me sit down next to her. She started to kiss my neck, her hand between my legs, and I felt her hot tongue delve into my ear, boiling me from the inside out. She said something but I couldn't hear her over the racket the storm was making, because the fury inside me was growing too, searching for new expressions, taking root and climbing up my torso, and the hotter I was the more firmly Analí squeezed me with her hand, the more I wanted her the more I detested her, and then we began to take off each other's clothes, gasping and greedy, and when I put my hand in her knickers she was wet and warm and my resentment went in a different direction, overflowing into something else. I turned her over on the bed and she let herself fall onto her front. In that position, her head buried in the mattress and her buttocks raised, I mounted her from behind, grabbing her waist to slide myself all the way in, and while the thunder rolled, the clatter of rain beating me inside, I rammed into her again and again with a force I didn't know I had, not looking at her, eyes fixed on the Swiss meadow on the wall, its sky reddish in the candlelight, time swelling, dilating, swelling again inside the hut, Analí's distant moans getting further and further away, fading and then coming back again, so close now, resounding inside me until, with a cry, they dragged me from this world and everything in it.

I woke up, a long time later, to the sound of a bird chattering. I noticed the light coming in through the gaps in the woodwork. I turned onto my side and saw Analí asleep, curled up, hugging herself. I felt bad – that is, I felt that something was bad, terribly bad – and I got up to put on my trousers which were lying on the floor, my sweaty shirt, stuffing my feet as best I could into my boots. I opened the door to the hut and was blinded by the sun outside.

My eyes were still adjusting, and I thought for a second that was why there was such a bright reflection coming off the tanks. I rubbed my eyes, looked again, and my head filled with the purest silence.

The surfaces of the tanks were covered in trout, their fat silver bellies floating upwards. I shuffled over and had to hold onto the edge of the cement wall. Not a thing was moving in there, and without thinking about it I stuck my whole arm into the first tank, pushing the dead trout aside. But it was completely still underneath, too, except for one or two animals drifting about stupidly on their sides. I looked for the water pipe that fed the tank. It was completely dry.

The world started to spin. I felt like the forest was hurtling towards the clearing, and instead of vomiting I let out a belch from deep in my gut. That cleared my mind a bit, enough to think about Don Henrik, about what was happening, about what was about to happen. My blood started to pound through my body again. I ran up the hill through the forest, following the pipe to the spring. Halfway there I discovered an enormous branch had fallen across the pipe. A pool had formed where the water was bubbling up from the broken plastic. I looked up and saw the trunk of a cauba, scorched where the lightning had struck it. I waded into the puddle, water up to my knees, and put everything I had into trying to move the branch. I couldn't shift it even an inch.

Numb, I ran back to the clearing, unable to feel my feet, and found Analí by the tanks, rubbing her eyes as she contemplated the dead trout.

What happened? she asked in a voice from another world.

I pushed her out of my way as I made for the back of the hut, where I grabbed a plastic bucket and took it over to the tanks. I filled it with trout and started to make trips to the freezer, back and forth, again and again, but in no time at all it was full. The surfaces of the tanks were still crammed with fish.

They look dead, said Analí, and I turned to look at her, at her then at the trout, at the trout then back at her.

I stood there as she went over and prodded one of the floating creatures with a finger. The surface was so choked it barely moved.

I tried to breathe normally, but there wasn't enough air around, and went back into the hut. I found my phone on the floor, picked it up and felt like it was burning my hand. I looked for Don Henrik's number.

When I came out of the hut again a strange, hot, prickling sensation was spreading over my skin. It was difficult to breathe. I could hardly move.

He's coming, I managed to say to Analí.

Who?

He's on his way.

Who?

She looked at me confused, raising a hand, demanding something.

Aren't you going to tell me?

The boss, you witch! I screamed at her.

She put her hands on her belly and held them there, together, very still, without saying anything. Regret ripped through my insides. After a while she lowered her gaze and, turning, headed off in the direction of the path. She was the second woman to walk away from me in two days. I raised my hands to my face, wanting darkness. Squeezing my eyes tight shut, I asked for everything to go back to how it was before. *Just like it was before*, I repeated, *just like it was before*. I opened them again and no one was there. For a couple of delicious seconds I gazed at the path, a place that was exactly the same as it had been for months. Eventually I turned to look at the tanks. The trout were floating on the surface.

★

The journey from the capital to San Agustín takes two hours. From there it's another hour and a half up the mountain to the farm. I waited for Don Henrik sitting on the edge of the first tank, the trout behind me. I couldn't bear to look at them. Every now and then I thought I heard the engine of the 4x4, could almost see it entering the clearing, the tyres sliding over the mud and then braking a few metres from where I sat, Don Henrik jumping down from the front seat and heading towards me. But the sound passed, the wind disappeared back into the trees, and the forest itself went silent, as though trying not to burst out laughing.

The clouds came over the mountainside again, and the sun poked its head out once in a while, filling the clearing with a white light that made me close my eyes. I opened them to look at my hands, unsure whether it was them or me or the world that was shaking. Eventually I stood up and managed to go for a walk.

The sky had cleared and an intense light brought out the green across the whole grove. I remembered my daughters up by the hut, their faces serious as they watched me work the tanks. My wife, my Ermiña, might not be my wife anymore. And Anali would be in her shop, or who knows where, hating me, maybe missing me a little.

I looked at the tanks and began to forget about the lump in my throat. The light fell directly on the trout, bouncing off their silver bellies, a bluish-purple glow rising off them like steam. It wouldn't be long before the place began to stink. Give it a couple of hours and the rooks would come, and the vultures, maybe even a quetzal. They'd sit in the surrounding trees, readying themselves for this great offering.

Welcome back, Don Henrik, I thought, and smiled, on the verge of tears.

I clasped my hands behind my neck, gripping it tightly, and waited for the boss to arrive.

DIVE

The thing is, he had a huge heart. I reckon that's why he was able to hang on for so long, Henrik said, because of that big heart of his. You think I'm tall, but my brother was half a head taller still. He took a beating, though. Imagine doing that many drugs for so many years – it'd destroy anyone. But Mati always had that air of youth about him, Henrik sighed, through all the lapses and relapses, even when what came crawling out of the gutter was no longer my brother but a stinking rag.

Amazing how much a body can change. I should know, I've carried Mati down this city's grimmest alleys. Passed out in a corner of the market, all swollen and barefoot. More than once it was me who had to get him out of there, and I'm telling you, it got easier and easier to carry him down those alleys. Drink makes you bloated, but the drugs made him lose so much weight there was only a bag of bones left to throw over my shoulder. On one of those trips from the station, when I'd already given him up for dead, he opened his eyes very wide and looked at me with that smile I told you about before, the one he'd had ever since he was a kid and that could win anybody over.

The lake trip I was telling you about was after Christmas. Mati had graduated from high school the year before – I remember exactly when, because he'd just pulled one of his little stunts. You know he used to disappear for two, three, four weeks at a time, sometimes more. But it was already December and we hadn't seen him for a month, so my parents decided the three of us would spend Christmas in Antigua. When we got back to the city, my mum turned on the lights and we discovered in the middle of the garden the old ceiba, same as always, except it had been turned into a Christmas tree. Mati had taken all the shoes out of our wardrobes and used them to decorate it. There were shoes right at the top, I've no idea how he managed it. My trainers were hanging off a twisted branch, and on another one further over I could see a pair of my mum's heels dangling precariously. She stood for a while looking at it all and then turned and went into her room. But my dad stayed there contemplating the tree, trying to decipher some meaning in the decorations, I guess, and when he turned to look at me he said, well, doesn't look half bad, does it?

That was the kind of thing my brother used to do. Not long after that, things started going downhill, but back then his antics still revealed a sort of wild, boundless affection. The next day he came by the house to give us a hug and say happy new year, though it wasn't actually New Year yet, and nobody mentioned the ceiba. There we were, only yards from our new Christmas tree, right there on the other side of the window, but my brother didn't mention it – he'd probably forgotten – and no one else brought it up. We had eggs and my mum's *smørrebrød* for breakfast. After they'd finished their coffee my brother took my dad into the study where he kept him talking for ages. On the other side of the table, my mum took little sips from her cup and avoided my gaze. We knew it was only a matter of time before the old man caved and gave him some money. When they came out of the study Dad looked at the floor, pleased to have Mati's hand on his shoulder, and it made me sad to see him like that, ashamed and happy all at once.

Mati went to stay at Tavo's house by the lake. Tavo was his partner in crime back then. He later killed a guy down on the coast and wound up in trouble with some bad people. But at the time my brother and Tavo were thick as thieves, thicker than thieves, because they'd egg each other on over the stupidest things, always needing to one-up each other. The night they arrived at the lake, Tavo got the idea to go into town looking for hookers to bring back to the house. They picked two up near Avenida Santander and Tavo, jumpy from all the drugs, started trying to be smart, talking tough, playing the hard man, and the whores said less and less, and looked at one another more and more. At some point, a knife appeared out of the back seat, up against Tavo's throat, and then the car went silent. A mile down the road the hookers got out, each one with a wallet in her hand. That was one of the stories doing the rounds back then: the time Tavo and Mati were mugged by a pair of hookers.

That was the night of the 30th, and they decided to shake it off by throwing a wild party at the lake house. I've been in the living room of that house, I've seen the huge window that opens out onto the garden, the lawn sloping gently down to the shore. The view of three volcanoes in the distance is so beautiful it almost hurts. Drugs aren't my thing, you know that, but if I had to pick a place to get high I'd say there, in front of that living room window. That would be the perfect place. They chose well, the bastards, and they had their party. Years later my brother would wind up begging for surgical spirits from the pharmacy in Zone 3, but back then he was still riding high on the wave, teetering right on the crest. The two of them must have looked rough as the lake in December by the time they had the idea to go diving. Only someone that high could think of going so low. Tavo told me later that they weren't drunk, and that anyway their minds were perfectly clear, with that clarity you get when you've been tripping for a while. The thing is, Tavo was an experienced diver, a licensed diver, but Mati was just a boy, a boy riding on the crest of the wave, keen to get to the bottom of everything.

Around that time a load of Mayan ceramics had been discovered on the eastern shore of the lake, around Santa Catarina Palopó, and there was a lot of talk about a submerged Mayan city. People round there had found bits of pottery on the beach with red and ochre designs, and they reckoned there'd been a ceremonial site on an island near the shore. But the water level had risen, drowning it all. That would have been hundreds, probably thousands of years ago.

I can imagine exactly how it all looked that morning, because I've seen it myself. You've got the three huge volcanoes on the other side of the lake, the shore skirting their flanks as it runs round the basin. At that time of day everything looks sharp but also very still. When the sun rises behind you the tips of the volcanoes start to glow and the light descends the slopes until it reaches the lake. It's so clear you can see everything that's going on in the water too – the fish in a morning daze, slipping lazily along the current.

Tavo decided they'd take the boat out, so they pushed off from the pier in front of the house in that amazing morning light. They followed the coast of Santa Catarina towards Agua Escondida. Obviously they both thought they knew exactly where the submerged city would be, but because they couldn't agree they decided to drop anchor somewhere in between. That's how they used to settle their differences – they were always good at that, you know. In the still-purple sky high above them, my brother spotted three stars in a row. This upset him, according to Tavo, though it's hard to know for sure what exactly it was he'd seen. Tavo says he refused to put on the diving kit after that. My brother had always felt connected to nature, to country life, and I think that's why he was mistrustful of manmade things, of any instrument that got in the way of that closeness. So Tavo put on his kit, did all the necessary checks, and dropped backwards into the water. Mati took a while longer, but before long he was in too, wearing a mask and snorkel.

It's cold, that lake – you know what it's like in December. But they probably had plenty of fuel in the tank, the kind of energy you get from drugs. Tavo went down about twenty feet and my brother followed him from above like a pilot fish, looking at everything his friend pointed to with the little trident he was holding. As they went on they reached a ravine where the lakebed dropped away sharply into darkness. They changed direction and skirted along the edge of the cliff instead. My brother dove down from time to time, looking more closely at the rocks and fish Tavo kept pointing out with his trident. On one of these descents he found that Tavo had stopped and was looking closely at a stone sticking out of the fine sand near the edge of the drop. He came up to breathe and, after taking a big lungful, dove down again.

They spent a few seconds looking at the stone. Tavo took out his mouthpiece and offered it to my brother. That way they could stay down there longer, passing the mouthpiece back and forth while they admired what looked like the upper part of a Mayan stela. After a while they moved closer and began to scrape away at the surrounding sand. The stone was smooth, Tavo said, hard and smooth, with carved inscriptions that they traced with their fingertips. As they did so, the lines became more visible, revealing the beginnings of a pattern that extended down beneath the sand. There was a design here, they'd be able to see it soon, Tavo thought, and continued digging at the sand around it. At some point he realised he was the only one working and looked up to find my brother at the edge of the ravine. He was staring, Tavo said, down into the darkness below. He wasn't moving and Tavo thought about going over to offer him the mouthpiece, but my brother looked so focused, so intent on the darkness, that Tavo stayed where he was by the stela. Then Mati turned and looked over his shoulder at him. This left Tavo cold, he told me, because he realised that *something fucked up was about to happen*, and he watched apprehensively, as, almost in slow motion, Mati's feet reached for the sand below him. Once he'd found solid ground he bent his knees and pushed off hard for the surface. It took Tavo a second to understand that Mati was going all the way up, that he was about to ascend without a stop. They'd been breathing the compressed air from the tank, and Tavo knew that air would expand as he rose, growing inside my brother's body until it burst his lungs. He needed to decompress, slow down his ascent, but details like that didn't figure into Mati's trip. Tavo let go of the stone and began his own ascent, exhaling continuously in emergency decompression, trying to do the least possible damage.

On the surface Mati was floating face up. Tavo pulled off his mask and my brother's too. His pupils were enormous, he told me. The veins in his neck were blue and swollen, creeping up from his chest to his face like an obscene version of the foliage on the stela. He wasn't responding. Tavo was talking to him but my brother just floated face up with his eyes wide open. Who knows how he managed to get him into the boat – imagine what that must have been like with a body like Mati's. But it's moments like these when you realise what friendship really means, when you've no choice but to have nerves of steel. Somehow Tavo managed to pull him up over the edge of the boat and sped off at once towards the public pier in Santa Catarina Palopó.

I went to that pier myself a few weeks later to ask people there what had happened. The fishermen said the launch came in so fast it almost smashed into the pier – a couple of them barely had time to get their cayucos out of the way. What surprised them most was my brother's neck, they said. It had swollen up so much it wasn't really there anymore, as if his body had grown right out of his head. He was a lizard man, said the guy describing him, blue veins running across his whole torso.

People crowded round the pier when they heard Tavo shouting. Soon the town ambulance arrived – a jeep turned emergency vehicle. Between a few of them they managed to get my brother onto a stretcher, but it was too long and didn't fit inside the jeep. In the end they got it in at an angle but had to leave the back door open to make space. Tavo said that all along the main road people were crossing themselves as the jeep went past, two bare feet bouncing up and down over the edge of the open back.

I was in the garden at home when the phone rang. I heard a scream, and then another, and when I went into the living room my mum was on the floor. My dad was trying to comfort her, on his knees beside her. It was strange: the first time in my life I'd seen them like that, from above, their bodies bent in distress. When he saw me my dad stood up and brushed the dust off his knees. Mati's in a bad way, he said. From one moment to the next, my hearing went. As though from very far away, I heard my dad mention something about my brother's lungs, a decompression chamber in Miami, that we had to get him there so they could fix him. Fix him? I asked, but my dad just looked down and put his hand on my mum's shoulder. On the floor, she was clutching her head in her hands.

That was our last family trip. My dad called a couple of his friends – fair-weather friends, as it turned out – and one of them contacted someone they knew who had a plane. That was what it was like in those days: people knew people who had planes. This guy agreed to rent us his little jet with its pressurised cabin, for a modest price that would contribute to my family's future financial ruin. So there we were, in the middle of the runway, waiting with a doctor and my brother on the stretcher. He was covered up with a sheet, wearing an oxygen mask, tubes coming out of his body. The doctor told us that nothing was certain, that once we got to Miami we'd have a better sense of what the options were. The pressure up there would be a problem, he said, pointing at the sky.

He was right. We hit a storm and the pilot had to ascend to forty thousand feet to get above the clouds. And that meant he had to increase the cabin pressure. The doctor told my dad he wouldn't be able to handle it, no sir, the pressure would be too much for his lungs. They're going to burst, the doctor started to say. He's going to burst, he repeated more loudly. We waited, gathered around my brother, in the jet's refurbished cabin, asking ourselves how much his body could take. My dad shouting at the pilot to decrease the pressure, the pilot shouting back that he couldn't unless he wanted the rest of us to explode instead. And so on we went, bucking on the black clouds, the pilot balancing precariously, the doctor sweating, the three of us resolutely gripping the stretcher, suspended, floating in that strangest of places, waiting for the storm to pass.

OUT OF THE BLUE, PERLA

It was the sugarcane harvest and the fields were burning. You could see flames all the way from here to the mountains. Ash floated around all day, sticking to your skin, your moustache, your eyelashes. We were all black with it. On the fifth day it rained. It doesn't rain in December, but that year it rained three days non-stop. The fields flooded, half-mud, half-ash. Nobody was working, nobody was cutting the cane. Those were strange days. That was when Perla was born – Perla, the cow who wanted to be a dog.

In my first drawing of Perla the cow, she appears in profile. Behind her, everything's plastered with ash; her smile flashes bright and clear against the darkness. What do you think? I asked my son once I'd given it the finishing touches. He looked at the drawing and then turned to me with that face that reminds me of his mother. Don't start getting attached, Dad, he said. It's a cow. And with that he went out to cut the cane with the other workers, and left me tracing over her tail with a piece of charcoal.

Perla's mother didn't want her. From day one she refused to let her suckle. Perla would approach, gently as can be, and her mother would shove her away with a swing of the hips. Bam! and off little Perla would go. She began to lose weight. I noticed right away and took her over to other cows who had calves, but none of them wanted her either. I went to talk to the boss. She needs a bottle, I told him, one of those huge ones, so I can give her some warm milk. The boss, Don Henrik, looked at me askance, but he trusted me. Within two days I was feeding her, letting her suck on an enormous bottle that she gulped from eagerly.

We tried to put her back with the others, but Perla didn't get on with the herd and the herd didn't get on with Perla. Don Henrik was sympathetic. Bring her to the garden at the hacienda, he said. We'll look after her there. And it was there that Perla met Blue, the mongrel who'd appeared out of the blue on the farm a couple of years back. They were instant pals. Pure chemistry. Nothing romantic, though, they were just friends. How they played, how they chased around in that garden, Perla and Blue.

She learned to stand on two legs, after seeing Blue do it so often. The spitting image, if you ask me. Because she even did the same little dance to keep herself upright, moving one little foot forwards and the other back, one forwards, one back. It's a strange sight, a calf balancing on two legs. They'd spend the whole day together, laughing together even. Don't ask me how, but whenever I came up to the garden and spotted them in the distance I swear those two rascals would be killing themselves laughing.

We grew melons on our farm, but it was surrounded by expanses of sugarcane fields belonging to the plantation. My son worked those fields, him and all the other day labourers. The work was hard, hacking away with a machete all day, spurred on by pills handed out by their supervisor. Amphetamines, that's what he used to give them. By the time they got home their pupils would be enormous. You can see those eyes, those wild pupils, in a portrait I did called *Son, again*, though my son wasn't happy with it. It's so ugly, Dad. He took it badly. Held it away from him, pinching just the edge. I told him it wasn't the drawing's fault: blame your mother and me, don't blame the art. He let go of the drawing, let it fall to the floor, and left my hut without another word. Those pills have robbed him of his sense of humour.

The plantation workers used to pass by our farm at the end of the day, on the way back to their shacks. That's how they became fond of Perla, who used to come out into the garden to greet them. They were all puffy from work and from those pills, but Perla would wag her tail, smile at them, stand on two legs to send them on their way. Dance, they'd tell her. Dance, shouted anyone with energy to spare, and Perla would reward them with a little step to the front, a little step to the back, another to the front, another to the back.

In any case, Perla started to grow. In less than a year she was full-size. She'd still go out onto the terrace to rest, legs splayed, nose flat to the bricks, eyes squinting in pure pleasure. She loved being scratched behind the ears and would moo gently if you showed her some affection. Blue would throw himself down next to her, the two of them adopting the same position. They were still pals, but when they played rough and tumble you could tell the dog was more careful, wary of Perla's heft. The cow didn't stand on two legs much anymore, she was too big for that now, but she'd still give the funniest little jumps.

The same year that Perla stopped growing, the first mechanised harvesters arrived at the plantation. They did the work of a hundred men in half the time. How they hacked away, those miserable machines, how they cut through the sugarcane with their steel blades. From one day to the next they started letting workers go, but the union stood firm and by the end of the year all hell broke loose. They chose the harvest period to put down their machetes and go on strike, marching together through the cane fields.

They went past the hacienda garden that day, everyone rowdy, both young and old, my son marching and yelling along with the rest of them. This was Perla's moment to shine. She jumped neatly over the hedge to be among the crowd, mooing in the friendliest way and letting everyone pet her. She wagged her tail, nodded her head up and down and mooed for the sheer joy of it.

It was finally clear, the thing we'd all suspected: Perla had sided with the workers.

The months that followed were pretty rough. People started to set fire to the new machines. They got hold of the first one in January, on a night when a whole warehouse went up in flames. You could see them from here, and the sirens sounded like the sugarcane itself was wailing at the top of its lungs. Don Henrik was staying on the hacienda at the time, and he went out onto the terrace to see what was going on. The two of us stood there very quietly, within the shelter of our own farm. You stay here with me, he said. Don't even think about getting involved. I wasn't totally past it yet, but most of my protesting days were behind me. I'd given enough of myself to the union in the city. It was my son's turn to put up a fight. The flames lit up the night: in the darkness I spotted Perla's shining gaze, her eyes dazzling in the firelight.

What happened next was only a matter of time. The mill owners brought in people from out east to patrol the sugarcane. These were bad people. Not that I've got anything against easterners, but these guys had murderous old mugs. It wasn't long before the union leaders started to fall. They shot two of the top guys, right there in their own huts. They killed the son of a third, just a kid who'd got himself mixed up in everything. So it looked like that would be the end of the whole mess, after those three hits happened in the space of just a few days.

My drawings from that time are pretty murky – it's like the charcoal itself was pissed off with the blank page. Perla's the only one I've got a good likeness of, her smile and energy anyway, because that cow was unusually restless, coming and going more like a dog than a heifer.

By the time some guys formed a Torch of Justice to put right all their grievances, people were already talking about breaking the strike and going back to work. There'd been food shortages. But the rumour about the Torch spread like fire in an open cane field: there's twenty of them, a few more maybe, poor wretches all of them, people started to say, but they're finally evening the score.

Ghosts, that's what they were like. Because the poor bastards would run back and forth through the sugarcane, materialising with their torches and then vanishing a split second later, leaving nothing but fire and chaos. The hired guns would leave by one side of the farm and the Torch would appear on the other: they stole fertilizer, jammed the machines in the mill, set fire to the mechanised harvesters. The mill was hit hard that season, what with so many fires and break-ins.

I knew who they were because of Blue. That dog had a couple of friends among the sugarcane cutters; I suppose in the end he was a card-carrying member of the Torch of Justice himself. He was faithful, Blue: faithful to chaos, because he had mischief in his soul. His coat was a cinnamon colour but he started to turn up in the mornings completely black, covered in mud from nose to tail. Only his teeth were white, and the little scamp would shoot me a look of pure glee. Blue, I'd shout, but before I could catch him he'd already be off into the undergrowth.

One night of a full moon, I heard the patter of his

paws. I could always tell it was Blue because he had a bad leg and lolloped as he ran. When I went out to have a look, he was arriving with two of those down-and-out torch bearers, him leading the way: that good-for-nothing had brought them back to the boss's hacienda. It took me a second to realise that one of them was my son. They went straight into the woodshed opposite the garden terrace to hide.

By the time the hired guns arrived everything was quiet; all I knew was we needed to keep a low profile. These guys were pissed off, wanted to hammer a lesson into those wretches. And there was no sign of the boss, no one else to see them off.

Fucking Blue, I thought. And that fucking son of mine. Fucking sugarcane, I thought too.

When I left my hut the gunmen were already cutting the wire fence, ready to bring their horses onto the farm. What do you want? I asked as I went out. This is private property. The first gunman didn't even bother answering. With one cut he severed the wire, and as they came in he just said: If we find them here it won't be pretty for you either.

Some of them circled the hacienda, but their leader just got down off his horse and stood there. Taking his time. And then his body tensed like barbed wire. I turned to see what he was looking at and saw Perla emerging from somewhere in the garden. Quick and sprightly she ran, heading straight towards him.

She was beautiful, that beast, I've never said she wasn't, but under the full moon she shone like a saint at Easter. So white she glowed. Flirty, friendly − so much personality. That was Perla. She got so close to him, and so confidently, that the leader seemed to lose his composure, and took a step back. If his men hadn't been there, I'm pretty sure he would have actually drawn his weapon.

But Perla was a cow, and there's no need to be afraid of a cow.

A few feet away she stopped. A couple of the gunmen came over and looked at her. Perla lowed at the sky and started to circle them familiarly, the cheeky thing. One of the men said something, his words harsh, but the rest were quiet, as curious as I was. Because Perla was giving them a look that was entirely human. And it wasn't the sort of look just anybody could give: it was the look a woman gives when she knows she's being looked at by a man. One of those women who snatches your gaze and slaps it right back at you. That's the look Perla was giving them.

What the hell's this? one of the guys started to say.

She didn't even give him time to finish. She stopped and looked him squarely in the face. Perla against them, Perla against the world. She took a couple of steps backwards and with a single push raised her whole body up: she made it look easy, so serene was she. Now she appeared to be balancing on two legs, resting her weight on her heels. And then she took two little steps forwards and the men retreated, ceding ground. She fell softly, Perla, like a sheet.

Frigging circus, one of them said. I have to admit: I felt a warmth in my belly that spread throughout my body – pride, or something like it.

It's her garden, I said, going over. The leader turned to look at me, then back at Perla. What do you mean, hers? She's special, you see, I said, she doesn't like people coming into her garden. The leader spat on the ground and directed his guys towards the melon plantations, the hacienda, the shed. Search properly, he told them. And you stay here, granddad. I don't care whose garden this is.

Those eastern guys were tough, hardened. They

knew about livestock, but I'm sure they'd never in their lives seen a cow lift herself up like that. They combed the area and left by the other side of the farm; in the meantime I focused on fixing the wire fence. I glanced around but my son and the other poor bastard were nowhere to be seen. They must have managed to sneak out during all the commotion. On the way back to my hut I found Blue with Perla. Huddled together like that, it was like they were having a conversation. I thought about giving the dog a good kick, but something stopped me; the two of them looked so at ease with each other, such good pals, their tails marking circles in perfect time.

The rumour reached me a couple of days later: that the Torch went everywhere accompanied by a dog and a demonic cow. The dog leading, the cow bringing up the rear. That the two animals would laugh together, having a ball, that they knew this land better than anyone. This cow and dog were always cracking each other up: leaping around the machines as they went up in flames, howling with laughter. That's what people said.

In any case: the gunmen came back a few nights later.

They were drunk and had me tied up in no time at all. Where's your missus? they asked. Where's your old lady? they shouted, laughing. But it was sour, perverted laughter. Hands behind my back and nose to the ground they had me, covered in mud outside the hacienda. I couldn't see much, but it was enough. The head honcho entered the garden and Perla ambled gently over, wagging her tail, still a bit dozy. The man scratched her behind the ear, patted her flank, and then gave the order: Fuck her, he said. Fuck her good and hard. I heard the cow lowing as they tied up her feet. Three of them held her still and another grabbed a log from the shed in the garden. It hurt my soul, listening to those moos – shrieks, really. As they were leaving, one of the guys came over and gave me a hefty kick. Don't worry about your mount, he said, she'll be exactly the same, she just won't be such a tease from now on.

It was a miracle she didn't bleed to death. I don't know what Perla felt – God only knows what that feels like, what an animal feels in a moment like that. But something in her died that night. Because she'd been flirty, Perla, she'd been proud, and they crushed all the grace out of her with that log.

The strike was called off a few weeks later. The workers secured some improvements – a small wage increase but little else. They stopped bringing in new harvesters, which only worked on flat ground anyway. Sometimes the ground won't flatten no matter how many times you run the field roller over it.

It wasn't long before our farm went bankrupt. The price of melons fell and Don Henrik had to sell everything. He talked to me, thanked me, gave my hand a good squeeze. That's life, he said. Really? I thought. I had no idea. The next day he got all the farmhands together to thank them and give the speech that would send them on their way. We listened in silence, me and the rest of them. And Perla? asked a voice from the back of the crowd. The boss looked down, shamefaced: what's left of the livestock will have to go to the slaughterhouse, he said. There are debts to pay. Behind him, in the garden by the hacienda, Perla wagged her little tail.

I ended up coming back to my hometown, only a couple of leagues from the farm. Here, I've been concentrating on my drawing, you wouldn't believe the hours I spend at it. I'm working on a couple of portraits of Perla, though I'm not sure about them yet. I've tried and tried but poor Perla always seems trapped in the picture, all stiff like. That's not how she was. My son and I agree on that, at least. You've even managed to ruin poor Perla with your drawings, he said when he saw the sketches.

I'm told Blue stuck around, coming and going through the sugarcane fields, doing his rounds. Occasionally he'd appear at the hacienda, converted into a warehouse now, and lie on the terrace in the garden. Right there, in the same spot where Perla used to throw herself down, he'd lie with his paws splayed and his nose to the bricks. Looking for company, I imagine, the kind of company you get from memories. Who knows whether he found it.

I reckon he did.

WHISKY

That night, Mati woke up to the dog whimpering. He shook off the sheets, damp with sweat, and walked barefoot to the kitchen. He could see the puppy through the darkness, whining by the window. He wanted to go out to the patio, that much was clear, but Mati stood on the threshold watching him. It sounds almost human, he thought. After a while he went over to open the door but stopped when he felt his foot splash through something wet. The smell of urine reached him a second later. He raised his eyes to the animal, now wagging his tail, and although it was dark he could have sworn he was smiling.

While he waited for the dog to pee outside, Mati opened one drawer after another until he found a pack of cigarettes. He'd been leaving them in different corners of the house – on kitchen shelves, in the bathroom cupboard, under the sink – and it gave him great satisfaction to stumble across one he'd forgotten. His sponsor had told him this wasn't a good idea, that this was the sort of behaviour that led to relapses, but then his sponsor had also given him the whiny dog. It had been three days already and he still hadn't come up with a name for the animal. He pondered it as he knelt to clean the floor, and kept thinking about it as he rinsed and wrung the cloth over the sink.

He opened the glass door and the dog turned to look at him, ears suddenly pricked up. There was a mocking glint in his eye, as though he knew something Mati didn't.

He sniffed the air around him, wagged his tail close to the ground and came over one little step at a time. When he reached the doorway he suddenly shot inside, slipping between Mati's feet. Mati closed the glass door, putting an end to the outing, and in that moment the name came to him. Whisky, he said very quietly, and then, turning to look for the animal in the darkness, repeated it more loudly: Whisky.

Mati's ex-wife arrived that Saturday to drop off their daughter. They'd agreed on a visitation schedule – two weekends a month – and Mati spent the entire morning tidying and cleaning the house. Since his recovery, he'd found cleaning to be surprisingly calming. If only his ex-wife could see him now, he thought, she might even take him back. Then he remembered the reasons why they separated. Grabbing the mop, he set about scrubbing the floor, paying attention to every single tile.

Pía was five years old and had a pink bow that she refused to take off even in bed. The bow had been a present from Mati, before his life had started to come apart at the seams, and seeing her in his doorway wearing it made him feel like his insides were being wrung out. But then Whisky appeared in the living room and the girl ran off towards the puppy, who immediately fled in terror. A couple of steps back from the door, his ex-wife eyed the inside of the house. Then her gaze fixed on Mati, noting the bags under his eyes, his crossed arms, the cigarette pack sticking out out of his shirt pocket. You look good, she told him, and Mati thanked her, but when she got to the car he saw her turn and look back at him. He knew that look.

Pía didn't leave Whisky alone the entire weekend. The puppy was delighted, even though he scarpered every time the girl let out one of her little shrieks. They took him for five walks in two days, and Pía demanded to hold the lead herself. They did lap after lap of the housing development, walking along the road by the ravine. It took Mati a while to figure out that what he was feeling was happiness, pure and simple, free of all those other emotions that accompanied him daily. He couldn't for the life of him get Pía to remember which house was his – they all look like yours, Daddy, she complained – and Mati was pleased to see her take after his ex-wife, even if that included her terrible sense of direction.

He began to look forward to his weekends with Pía and Whisky. Nothing changed about those visits except the size of the dog, who was growing at an alarming rate. He soon came across his daughter riding on Whisky's back, doing laps of the living room holding the animal's tail in one hand, convinced she was able to steer him. Giddy up, Whisky, giddy up! the child would cry. The dog would raise his head and off he'd go, proud as anything. Mati would sit in the armchair, leafing through a magazine but barely taking his eyes off his daughter, sure that in another life she must have been a princess and Whisky her trusty steed.

But Mati relapsed, despite the long dry streak, and from one day to the next he found himself propping up the bar, staring at a freshly brimming glass. He grabbed a fistful of dirty hair, clenching hard until it hurt. He thought, for a moment, that he was lost: that the glow would return – he'd watch, as though from a great distance, the burning wharves of the dead sea he carried inside him. He downed the rum in a single mouthful. With darkness came oblivion, and when, a couple of days later, he managed to open his eyes, he found himself at home, sprawled on the cold tiles of the living room floor. His sponsor was looking down at him with tired eyebrows. He helped him up and Mati sat on the armchair. His whole body hurt, and when he looked up he saw Whisky sitting in the opposite corner, his fur dirty and his gaze opaque. What might he have seen? The dog was so still, with a disinterest that bordered on insolence, that he looked like an old pagan god, an idol from a culture that owed Mati nothing.

The next day he was back in group meetings. He committed himself fully to recovery, thinking about his daughter's imminent visit that weekend. Pía arrived on the Friday with a little suitcase in one hand, wearing a beach hat that was too big for her. When Mati opened the door she threw herself at his leg and hugged it tightly. He put his hand on the girl's head. From somewhere in the house Whisky let out a howl and Pía shot off in search of him. Mati and his ex-wife stood face to face, and he didn't quite know what to do. He'd shaved that morning and for the first time in months had shined his shoes. Then he noticed she was wearing make-up – it was subtle, but still, she was wearing make-up – and was heartened when he thought he detected the sweet trace of her perfume. Don't forget her vitamins, she told him, handing him a Ziploc bag full of pills. They stood there a moment, not saying anything, until his ex-wife turned and went back to the parked car. See you Sunday, she said, raising a hand as she went.

What's up with Whisky? asked his daughter when Mati shut the door. How do you mean? Pía pointed and Mati looked at the dog: his fur had got its shine back and his eyes no longer seemed so resentful. He's happy, he replied, he hasn't seen you for days. The girl frowned, looked at Whisky and put a hand on his neck. It's like he's all dopey, she said, but rather than waiting for Mati to reply she knelt down and hugged him tightly. Whisky wagged his tail but Mati could see that, from down there, the dog continued to eye him.

That night they ordered pizza and ate in the little living room, Mati in his armchair and Pía opposite him on the folding chair he'd brought in from the patio. Whisky sat beside the girl, and Mati said nothing when he saw her quietly slip him a piece of crust. He knew then – without knowing why but with complete certainty – that Pía would grow up to be a good person, and that conviction transformed everything in the little living room from one moment to the next. The light from the bulb seemed to soften and breathe at the same time, the furniture became cosier and the tiled floor grew more solid, as though the private world of objects had conspired to shelter and protect his daughter.

They finished eating and Mati took the plates into the kitchen. He felt a barely contained euphoria running through him and knew he needed to calm down. Relax, he told himself, just relax. He asked Pía if she wanted to learn to play chess – he'd already offered a number of times with no success – and took advantage of the girl's silence to go and find the chessboard. He carried the folding chair into his room and put it down against the wardrobe. His hands trembled as he rummaged around on the top shelf, and as he tried to still them, he heard the yell. For a couple of seconds he remained motionless, trusting that his daughter and the dog were just playing, and when he didn't hear anything else he called to her. Pía, he called again, louder. Nobody answered, so he got down off the chair and left the bedroom. There was no one in the living room. He looked in the kitchen and went over to the patio, also empty, and then, turning to the front door and seeing it open, he heard another shout.

Pía was standing in the middle of the street, one hand clutched in the other, and Mati had a horrible premonition that this scene was going to repeat itself later in her life. Whisky, screamed the girl, her eyes full of tears. He's gone, Daddy, he's gone, she sobbed, turning to look at him. Mati looked up and down the street, the lines of identical little houses set shoulder to shoulder running in both directions. What happened? he asked, and Pía stretched out her hand, pointing vaguely. He ran out, I opened it to take him for a walk, and he ran out. Mati closed the front door and picked Pía up. With her in his arms, he walked quickly in the direction his daughter had indicated.

They circled the entire housing development, both of them yelling the dog's name over and over. The girl had her arms round his neck and he could feel her tears warm on his cheek. But Whisky didn't show up. After a while he had to put his daughter down and hold her hand until they got to the security lodge at the entrance. The guard put his hands up, wanting immediately to stay out of it. Nothing's come this way, he said. You sure he isn't hiding in the house? Mati looked at his daughter and then at the guard, and suddenly felt like punching him in the face. He studied the street opposite the housing development, which gave onto an avenue full of heavy traffic. Only then, still gripping his daughter's hand, did he feel a stab of anxiety.

He carried Pía back to the house and asked her to wait for him there, but she wanted to continue looking. If Whisky comes back, said Mati, someone needs to be here to let him in. Pía considered this, her cheeks red and clammy, and then nodded silently. Mati went out to walk the streets of the housing development, properly noticing every house for the first time. They were uglier than he'd thought, home to other fools like him convinced they were on the up though they were clearly in a downward spiral. If one of them's stolen Whisky... he thought, trying to see into the little windows of every façade. He headed down the street that skirted the ravine, shouting the dog's name until his throat started to burn. He stopped, and, taking a deep breath, clasped his hands behind the back of his neck. His palms were drenched in sweat.

There was nothing left to do but leave the development. He started to walk the neighbourhood's poorly surfaced streets, full of potholes, devoid of pavements, and felt certain that if Whisky had left there was no way he'd be able to get back. He thought of the thieves swarming the area, imagined gangs of sadistic children. He saw old people sitting on plastic buckets outside shops, doubtless criminals in the privacy of their own homes. After searching the nearby alleyways, he headed for the main avenue. From a corner he watched buses elbow cars out of the way, cars charging into motorbikes, motorbikes snaking through the chaos. All was smoke and clattering metal. He shouted the dog's name a couple more times with what little voice he had left, but could barely even hear himself.

When he got back to the house Pía looked at him with enormous eyes and immediately lifted her little hands to her face. She started to cry inconsolably, collapsing in on herself. She shook between hiccups and Mati had to take her in his arms. But the girl extricated herself and went over to Whisky's basket. She got inside it and cried herself to sleep. Mati made up her bed in the living room but couldn't bring himself to move her. When he finally went over to get her into her pyjamas, well into the night by this point, he could see her eyes moving worriedly beneath closed lids.

He got up early the next morning and found Pía awake, sitting in the basket again. He took her under the arms and stood her on her feet. I heard Whisky in the night, she said. He was barking. Mati knelt on one knee and straightened out her pyjamas, which were all rucked up. Where did you hear him? Really far away, said Pía, he was sad. We'll have to go out looking again, said Mati, and he got up to take a box of eggs out of the fridge. He broke three into a bowl and started to beat them, but his daughter wouldn't stop looking at him. Let's go, Daddy. Mati took the frying pan out of the cupboard and turned on the hob. Can't go out looking all day on an empty stomach, he said. Pía dropped her gaze, crossed her arms, and sat down in the dog basket to wait for her breakfast.

Outside the sun was strong and half a block away they had to turn back for Pía's hat. In the street they went from door to door. Mati thought of Whisky, of the lazy flick of his tail, the reverence with which he used to nose up to Pía. That dog was too good, he knew. The neighbours, previously invisible, were more helpful than he'd expected. But their encouraging words played against him: Pía was heartened by stories about extraordinary dogs who'd crossed half the world to get back to their owners. He watched her pick up the pace, knocking on doors with her closed fist. They walked on, increasingly sweaty. By the time the sun started to go down, Mati noticed that Pía was dragging her feet, her eyes fixed on the ground.

At home they made sandwiches. Pía hadn't said a word since they got back, but Mati noticed she was looking at him differently. Maybe it wasn't reproachful, he wanted to tell himself, only full of questions he didn't know how to answer. They ate in silence and soon Pía was fast asleep in the armchair. Mati took the opportunity to call his sponsor, whose car would help broaden their search area. I'm out of the city, he replied, I can't get back until Monday. Mati murmured his thanks and after hanging up went out to the patio.

He smoked a cigarette, did one lap of the cement quadrangle and lit another one. He remembered how Whisky used to jump in excitement when he got his bowl out. He'd tried to train him not to, not to rest his front paws on people's thighs, but never succeeded. He could picture the dog's face after a smack on the nose, his expression hurt but then immediately cheerful again, wagging his tail, nervous and grateful at the same time. He was overwhelmed with regret. He'd never hit him again. Whatever happens, he thought, I'll never hit him again. He wanted to stay out on the patio, spend a little while with the memory of his dog, but Whisky's presence was slipping away from that space. As he stubbed out his cigarette he heard something behind him. He turned and, seeing Pía's silhouette among the shadows of the kitchen, opened the glass door.

The girl had just woken up and her hair was all rumpled, a couple of strands stuck to her sweaty forehead. She still wasn't properly awake and looked at Mati without seeming to recognise him. There was something disconcerting in her face. Pía, he said, but the girl just looked at him unblinking, her face dark, disdainful even. Pía. He felt the hair on his arms stand on end. He wanted to reach his hand out to her but didn't dare. Pía, he repeated, and the girl turned to look behind her with an almost animal movement, attentive to the shadows in the kitchen, to the shadows in her dreams, to the world she'd left behind but that was only just beginning to fade.

A second later, his daughter was back. Tipping her head to one side, she looked at her dad in some distress. Is Whisky back yet? Mati bent towards her, looking into her face, and gave her a hug. Not yet, Pía. He leaned back a little so he could see her properly. His heart was beating hard and his mouth was dry. But I'm sure we'll find him, he said. Feeling dirty, deceitful, he squeezed his daughter to him. After a while he got up and breathed the cool night air. The girl looked at the sky. We have to tell Mummy, he heard her say. Mati lit a cigarette, giving himself time to reply. Let's find him first, he said. If we tell her there'll be more of us, the girl responded, and Mati took another drag and blew the smoke out hard. Pía's hand reached for him, tugged on his shirt. If we want to find him, it's better to tell Mummy.

They agreed to wait until the next morning to call her, and Mati felt like an enormous clock, a clock of cosmic proportions, had begun counting down. He imagined his ex-wife's tired greeting, saw her enter the house, take in his sparse furnishings, walk across the tiny kitchen to the patio and realise that was it. He knew the expression she'd be wearing when she turned to look at him, he'd seen it too many times. He looked at himself in the mirror as he washed his hands in the bathroom, and thought about his own expressions, his ways of hiding or revealing the things that happened to him, as though they were happening to somebody else.

They spent the rest of the night in the living room. Pía couldn't sleep and Mati realised that he didn't know what to do with his daughter, how to pass the time now that Whisky's absence had carved a hole in their day. He remembered one of the children's books he used to read her, about a dragon that had fallen in love with three princesses. He went to look for it and when he returned to the living room he found his daughter nodding off. After helping her into her pyjamas, he picked her up to lay her in the camp bed and covered her with a blanket. As he waited there, he knew that something shadowy was coming in his direction. He went to his room and sat on the edge of the bed. He felt the tingling in his fingertips, the surging tide that would drown everything. He clutched his forehead in one hand, let out a deep groan, breathed deeply, let out another one. But the pressure didn't ease. He knew where he needed to go, the exact distance to the throbbing hubs of the city where he'd find relief. He got up, went to the living room and stood next to Pía again. He looked at the front door. His hands were sweating – a switch had flicked inside him. He went out to the patio, rested his forehead against the wall. Banged it three times, harder and harder. He stepped back, dizzy, feeling his brain reverberate. He tried to light a cigarette, took a big drag then let it fall to the ground. He went back to the living room. Desperate, he grabbed the dragon book and took it into his room. He tried to read, but the words had only one meaning, pointed only in one direction, and Mati wanted to clasp the dragon's tail and fly away from there, the wind roaring around him. He lay back on the bed and covered his face with the open book. His heart was clamouring, his own breath damp and hot against the pages. He balled up the sheets in his fists and trusted, with no hope at all, that the storm would pass.

He didn't know how long he'd been there. At some point he felt something warm against his arm. He let go of the sheet, which he was still clutching, and pushed the book off his face. Pía was standing by the bed, holding onto his wrist. I can hear Whisky, she said. Mati looked at the window and saw that it was still dark. His shirt was soaked with sweat. He's barking, Daddy. Mati put his hand on the girl's head, asking himself if Whisky's bark would haunt her for the rest of her childhood, in the same way certain ghosts had accompanied him for years. I know, Pía, I hear him too sometimes. The girl's eyes widened. Then let's go, Daddy! Mati got up with some difficulty, passing a hand over his face, and nodded. He'd lain down with his shoes still on, so only needed to get Pía into a jumper and then they were ready.

Outside everything was very dark, and they had to go back to the kitchen for a torch. As they went out again he thought he heard something. He waited a couple of seconds, holding Pía by the shoulder, but all was quiet. The girl turned to smile at him, her eyebrows raised. You heard it too? Mati looked at her, at both sides of the street, and his body gave an involuntary shudder. He should have put on a jumper too. Where do you want to look? he asked his daughter, and the girl pointed to the right without hesitation. He locked the door, and after a few steps heard another noise, similar to the first. But it couldn't be. He walked with Pía in the direction she'd chosen and his daughter took the lead, heading down the middle of the road. The lampposts with neon lightbulbs, spaced out along the street, illuminated little patches with their dusty light. Pía turned to look at him – her finger pointing the way – and Mati felt like he'd already lived through this nightmare. Then he heard the bark. It was a thin thread of a bark, a long way away, but in the silence at that hour it couldn't be anything else. Whisky! shouted his daughter. She started running down the street beside the ravine, and Mati recalled, panicking suddenly, legends about damned souls that would howl to attract their victims. Pía, he shouted, shining ahead with the torch as his daughter disappeared into the darkness. Then he too began to run, and as he caught up with the girl he heard the bark again, a bark that could only be Whisky's. They slowed down as they approached the edge of the ravine. Mati asked Pía to wait there and went on slowly. He looked over the edge, but the torchlight was lost in the depths below. He shouted his dog's name and his dog responded. His barks were heavy with despair, more like laments, but they were Whisky's. Pía shouted back, and Mati too, and Whisky responded again. Wait here, Pía, wait here and I'll be right back.

The slope was steep, a few bushes clinging to the crumbling earth. Sliding, almost dropping the torch, Mati made his way down. On the other side of the ravine he could make out a feeble glow and didn't know if it was dawn breaking or the moon's dirty gleam. He lost his balance and before he knew it found himself tumbling downhill. If a spiky shrub hadn't broken his fall he'd have carried on all the way to the bottom. He lifted his hand to his head, which hurt, then stood up gingerly. When he touched his arm it burned intensely, and he couldn't find the torch. He heard Whisky's bark again, now much closer, and something else too. He listened carefully, and a putrid wave washed over everything. It was sewage water, the city's dark tears running deep in the ravine.

The descent became even steeper and he had to clutch whatever was to hand. He quickly realised that the bushes were nettles, because his hands were burning and his fingers didn't fit inside their skin anymore. He negotiated some undergrowth, trying to figure out the best route, but he couldn't find anywhere to put his feet. He shouted his dog's name and at that moment saw that down below, just a few yards away, something was moving. Whisky, he said again, and the animal's whimper cut through the warm foetid air. He approached the edge again and slid down to the bottom over the sandy earth, dragging part of the cliff down with him. He fell into the standing water on the sand, his shoes splashing, and managed to steady himself against some rocks that stood up like enormous prehistoric teeth. His eyes were beginning to adjust to the darkness when he saw the animal. He looked, for a moment, like a creature from another world, heading towards him with no regard for his surroundings. The water ran thinly over the sand, steep rockfaces either side of it, remnants of plastic containers forming islands in the stream. The creature edged slowly towards him, making a sound that wasn't exactly animal. Mati knelt down, holding onto a rock, the warm water soaking his trousers. He held a hand out in front of him and waited, his heart in his mouth, terrified and full of hope for their reunion.

UBALDO'S ISLAND

That's where they came in, says Ubaldo, pointing to the coconut grove in the distance. They came off the road down to the beach, through that scrubland, to where we're standing now. There were a bunch of them, he says, looking at Andrés, eight or nine, and all of them were armed when they got out of the 4x4s. Well, all except the lawyer anyway.

With the big toe of his left foot, Ubaldo draws circles in the dark sand. Andrés, you know I want to do right by the boss. But when when you're faced with weapons like that, he says, looking up, things start to take on a whole different calibre. Ubaldo's eyes are greyish, a bit like the dirty sea crashing on the beach. They sat me down just there, he said, pointing at the table under the thatched canopy, and started telling me about your stepdad, Andrés, about the boss. Well, they didn't all talk: some of them circled the house, others stationed themselves under the canopy. Only the lawyer was here to talk.

Andrés takes two beers out of the blue icebox and helps himself to one of them. He leans back in the hammock and gestures to Ubaldo to drink the other, but Ubaldo just opens the can and waits, listening for a while to the sea, to the waves breaking and retreating along the beach. Finally he takes a swig of his beer, puts it on the floor and in the same movement slides down into his hammock.

It was complicated, he says from there.

An hour and a half the lawyer kept me. I was squirming, wriggling like an eel, trying to keep him happy. Taking a hard line would have been ugly. He said your stepdad was in debt, Andrés, that he couldn't keep his word, that's why they'd come, to chase up all his broken promises. Just sign, said the lawyer with a pen in his hand, sign here Ubaldo, practically stabbing me with the pen, because if you don't then you'll be the one who's let us down. But you know I don't own this land, I told the lawyer, the boss does. I wish I could sign. I just live in the hut next door, I just look after the house and fix the thatch, who am I to sign away the land?

The lawyer was angry, Andrés, and clever, the bastard had an answer for everything. I wasn't to worry, it had all been arranged with the Registry Office, my signature was more than enough; he offered me money, a lot of money. Five thousand pesos, he told me, we'll pay you five thousand pesos, Ubaldo, all you have to do is sign and we'll look after you, you can keep your nice little job, your hut, plus five thousand pesos a month for looking after the land. The signature was just for show, Andrés, to make sure we weren't going to cause them any problems down here on the coast. The lawyer knew your stepdad couldn't afford to pay me a thing anymore, he knew all about the boss's tricky situation.

After stopping here they went on to other plots of land further down, and along the beach too, and there they asked some of the boys, the caretakers, to be their eyes and ears, to keep tabs on us. But those boys are from round here too, they're all from Monterrico – we knew they wouldn't give us away. Only one of them said yes, a kid from the highlands who looked after Don Vinicio Gutiérrez's beach house. A bit dim, that kid, I knew him – in Monterrico everyone knows everyone – but he was pretty slow, always had this cowardly look about him, and all it took was a few pesos before they had him under their thumb. I guess the kid didn't know better: here in Monterrico we look after our own, but he was from the highlands and hadn't figured it out yet, didn't know that if he took the money there'd be hell to pay.

I was up three nights in a row, Andrés, couldn't sleep after those men came to visit. It's grim, sleeplessness, having to keep vigil, feeling like you're asleep when actually you're numb with fear. Ubaldo points two fingers like a gun over the top of the hammock: I was getting into bed with one of these, he says, had it loaded by my pillow. Didn't let my wife and kids sleep at my place anymore either, sent them away because I didn't want them around with all this going on. You can't risk putting your family in the way of people like that.

He picks the beer can up off the ground and takes two big swigs from it. It's always been quiet round here, he says. His gaze moves from the sea to the coconut grove then back to the sea. We're surrounded by canals, Andrés, so this is actually an island, connected to the mainland but an island all the same. There are only two ways in: by crossing the bridge, the one you came over, or by getting a boat across the canal on the other side of the island. That way we stay informed, if someone's on their way we know about it.

They fall silent and the idea of being on an island seems to settle over things: everything is more precarious now, everything feels slightly adrift.

I talked to your stepdad, says Ubaldo, called his mobile as soon as the men left. My hand was shaking, and I'm no sissy, now, but in the middle of the call the phone started shaking against my ear. He took his time, you know what he's like, waiting quietly on the other end of the line, and when I finished he thanked me.

He didn't explain much, though his silence told me plenty. This is delicate, that's all he said, these people are dangerous, Ubaldo, I'm grateful for your support.

When he came to visit me the next day, straight from the capital, he brought a bodyguard who waited for him in the car. He shook my hand, firmly as ever, and we went to the beach to get a bit of fresh air. But there wasn't enough. I couldn't get enough air. Your stepdad couldn't either, I don't think, because he struggled to get the words out, to tell me about his business partner, the one who'd passed information to the gunmen. I'm sure he's told you some of this, Andrés, but right then, while he was telling me, he started to lose it. That son of a bitch, he started to say, which was strange because I've never in my life heard him tear into someone like that. My ex-partner, that son of a bitch: if we never got the business off the ground it was only because the buyers let us down. I didn't realise the kind of person he was till it was too late, he said. He knew some bad people, my ex-partner, people like him – the only difference was that what he did with a pen, they did with a gun.

They showed up at my office, your stepdad explained. There were a few of them. The guy who was in charge, plus the lawyer and a bunch of gunmen: three gunmen in my office. It was late. They came in the evening when there was no one around. Just me and my secretary: she let them in, went out to see who it was when they knocked. They tied her to a chair, were pretty rough with her. They pulled a gun on me in my office and sat me down. For hours. It felt like forever, Ubaldo, that was how long they held me at gunpoint: forever. The leader was wearing a wig and dark glasses he never took off. Demanded I sign over a bunch of accounts. IOUs too. And some company shares. That's why they brought the lawyer. The lawyer took care of everything, Ubaldo, he knew exactly what to ask for and how to find it. The leader just stood smoking, with his dark glasses and his wig, smoking, calm as you like. He wasn't in any rush, Ubaldo, just stood there dropping ash all over the office floor. In the end, when it looked like they were done, the leader says: And the little piece of land too, we know there's some land down on the coast. You can start making that over too, we'll be in touch so you can sign the deeds for us.

By the time they left it was dark. I felt awful about my secretary: she was scared stiff, frozen, poor thing. I untied her and she sat there very still. Mari, I asked her, are you alright, Mari? But Mari said nothing. Not until later, after I'd called Juan, a friend of mine who'd been a colonel. When Juan arrived he asked me not to touch anything and started talking to Mari. He eased her out of her shock. Stood her up, and between the two of us we helped her walk. I put my coat around her and we started walking in circles, just round the office, round in circles. Round in circles over the cigarette ash. Walking. Loosening her up. When Juan took her home later he told me what I already knew: don't involve the police in this. These guys are not to be messed with, I'll look into it for you, he said. And he has looked into it, he's still got contacts in high places. Juan's been a huge help, and basically, yeah, they were bad people, those guys who came to visit me.

Your stepdad stayed a while on the beach, says Ubaldo. I kept him company, the two of us sitting on the sand looking at the sea, but after that he didn't say much. Only that the colonel was helping him. Juan's a good person, he said, he knows people who can back me up: the guy I've got in the car, for example, he's someone Juan trusts. He goes everywhere with me now. Looks out for us at home. I take him to the office too. And Juan's guys come and visit: it's to make sure they're seen, Juan said, show those people you're not alone. Since all this happened I haven't heard from them again. Till yesterday, that is, till you called me yesterday, Ubaldo.

They came in from over there the second time, Ubaldo says to Andrés, pointing: a few days after your stepdad was here they showed up on the sand, but there was just one car this time. My guys had already warned me. They called when they saw them cross the bridge to say there were three of them on their way: the lawyer and his secretary and one gunman. I met them at my hut and the lawyer got out, all smiles, trying to seem friendly. I went along with it: got them a couple of beers. Even the gunman did alright for himself, waiting outside the hut, bottle in hand, while the lawyer, the secretary and I started talking.

Very friendly, the lawyer was, nothing but smiles. It was all: isn't this a nice property, isn't the hut so well looked-after. All: you can't find decent men anymore, except down here on the coast. Isn't that right, Jackelin? And Jackelin, who was sitting on the little chair with a folder on her lap said, you're right, boss, you can't beat a man from the coast. The lawyer nodded, pleased with her responses, coughed out a laugh or two, and then came out with it: we're in a bit of a tight spot, Ubaldo, we have a little problem and we need to sort it out. That's why I've brought Jackelin along, Ubaldo, she can help us work things through. I know you're not one for violence, I know that you'd rather talk it out, and that's why we've come with a peace offering. Through all this the secretary was looking at me intently, very serious and very focused she was, her legs crossed and her little black skirt clinging to her thighs.

They had a number of proposals, the lawyer said, options to help facilitate the matter, and all they needed was for me to be willing. Willing, he repeated: a bit of enthusiasm, that's all we need from you, Ubaldo. He looked at me a while, letting his words sink in, then took his phone out of his pocket. I'll be back in a bit, I have to make a call, take your time and we'll talk later. The lawyer went out of the hut and left me there with Jackelin, who was still looking at me intently. With her gaze alone she had me pinned to the spot. So there I was trying to waste time, trying to avoid her, even though I could already feel the heat in my body; I was like a schoolboy, even my hands were sweating. Her eyes were pressing at me all over, and it felt good, that pressure; you know what I'm talking about, Andrés.

At that point Jackelin stands up, skirt clinging a bit tighter to her thighs, and starts coming over to me. I felt the heat of her body, Andrés, felt my own heat as she got closer, looking around my hut with a little smile that pissed me off and turned me on at the same time. She took her time, playing with one of her curls while my body was getting me going. And that smile, always with that delicious fucking smile getting me all riled up. When she reached me she bent over a little, put her hand on my neck and brought her face next to mine, her words warm in my ear: that bed over there, it looks so inviting, Ubaldo, it would be so nice to lie down for a moment, don't you think?

I froze, because the bed was my son's. The one my wife and I slept in was next to it, but Jackelin had fixed on my son Brener's bed. You probably know about the condition Brener's had since he was a baby, the disease that almost killed him: that's why I owe your stepdad so much, Andrés, he always helped me out, taking us to hospitals, calling the doctor, buying us pills. He never charged me a cent, your stepdad. The same bed Jackelin was talking about, that was where Brener was so sick. That's my son's bed, I siad, my son who's been sick for a very long time. Jackelin kept looking at me. And then I said to her: that bed's been soaked through with my son's sweat. He almost died in that bed. That's all I said, looking right at her, holding her gaze, never mind how excited I was by her black eyes, Andrés, those black eyes inside my body, turning me inside out. And you know what? Jackelin's face started changing, not much but a bit, little changes, little things that can transform a person into someone different. She looked at me and looked at the little bed and suddenly it was a different Jackelin in my hut, no heat sweating out of her pores, no heat coming out of my pores, or if there was it had nothing to do with the arousal of a moment ago. She turned to look at the door, looked outside, and then leant down a bit more and said in my ear very quietly that I shouldn't worry. Don't worry about it. That's all she said, and then she padded quietly back to her chair, picked up the folder she'd left on the floor and put it back on her lap.

We waited in silence for a long time. At some point the lawyer stuck his head round the door. He peered in, had a good look, then slid his sweaty body into the shade inside. I take it you're not into women, then, he said loudly. Jackelin was sitting up straight in her chair, the folder very still, avoiding the lawyer's eyes. I said, Ubaldo, I take it you're not into women. I looked the lawyer in the eye and replied, calmly as I could: My wife is on her way, sir. Well, shall we wait for her then? I knew the sort of games these people played, I had the measure of them by then, so I just said yes, we could wait for whatever they wanted, she'd be back at some point tonight. The lawyer exhaled, exhaled slowly, and then put his half-empty beer on the floor. Ubaldo, he said, you're meddling in things that don't concern you. I'm just doing my job, I told him, what else am I supposed to do. We know your boss came to see you, the lawyer said, we've been told he was here two days ago, so don't go acting smart. Well, what am I supposed to do if he decides to show up? The lawyer pinched the front of his shirt with his fingertips and started to fan himself, looking outside: I know you care about your boss, Ubaldo, but I also know you care about your family. We want to help you with your son, we know he's been ill. We wouldn't want anything else to happen to that son of yours. My son is fine, I told him, he's healthy and well looked-after. And that's how we want him to stay, Ubaldo, healthy and well looked-after: do me a favour Ubaldo, all this nonsense, just cut it out.

I said nothing, trying to figure out where the gunman was. I had my .22 right beside me, under a cushion. I'm sorry, sir, but you'll have to discuss this matter with the boss, not with me. We can all talk about it, Ubaldo, you're involved in this too. The gunman had come to the doorway and was standing there quietly, hands on his waist. I recommend that you prepare yourself, Ubaldo, that you find the courage to do the right thing for you, the right thing for your family. When my boss comes, because it won't be long before he comes to see you, you're going to sign this deed. He stood up and went over to Jackelin and gestured for her to give him the folder. I'll leave you a copy, he said, so you can familiarise yourself with it, so you can see what it is you'll be signing.

With that he gave me the papers and walked out. Jackelin, he said as he was going, and Jackelin stood up with a little jump, not even looking at me, and walked out behind the lawyer. I sat there, my back drenched in sweat, and didn't leave my hut until I heard the car start up and go. The vehicle went off down the beach, back the same way it had come.

There was nothing else for it, Andrés: I went to talk to the others that same afternoon. On my way into town I dropped in to see family – went to my brother Milton's place and told him to come with me, then the two of us stopped by my cousin's house to tell her husband Ángelo, who joined us too, and finally to the canal, to look for my brother Tono, who's always fishing for prawns in the mangroves. There were four of us. My two brothers, Ángelo, and me. Tono, the prawn guy, counts for two, though: he's a proper man, huge, no stranger to a good fight. So the four of us headed into the centre of Monterrico and started rounding people up, trying to find those who mattered.

We got everyone together in the warehouse where they keep boats during the hurricane season. There were only two in there at the time, propped up against one side of the warehouse, and the rest of the place was empty. It felt enormous with the few people we'd gathered in there. Everyone already knew about the gunmen, about your stepdad's land. We want peace in Monterrico, I said to them, if they get a foothold on the island then we're all screwed. And everyone understood: that's all they said, that they understood, but that we couldn't go challenging people like that. I should just sign, a few of them said, the land wasn't even mine, it was the boss's. Me, they'd look after, but sticking their necks out for someone else's land was a whole other question.

You're lucky, Andrés, fortunate to have a stepdad like yours. Because the boss was always kind, never arrogant, unlike so many landowners round here, always said hi to people. If there's one thing people round here don't like, it's arrogance. There's plenty of that around. But your stepdad was never like that. Every now and then he'd go into town to have a few beers, always happy to buy a round, up for a good time at Doña Ester's beach bar. But he was always kind, always cheerful. If you ask me, that's what did it. Because there were people here who appreciated him, especially the women – they're the only ones who can keep their wits about them once the drinking gets going. They knew what he was like, his good nature, how respectful he was even when he'd had a few too many.

But that afternoon in the shed nobody was in a party mood, everyone was attentive and very serious, and it was there that Doña Ester stood up to defend your stepdad. She talked and then a few other women joined in, women who spoke quietly but firmly. They supported me and your stepdad both. Stop talking rubbish, they said, if even one gunman gets his way in Monterrico they'll all be here. How are we supposed to protect our children; we've seen what happened further down the coast when gunmen got involved. Kids off the rails, everybody terrified, nobody consulted before decisions were taken. We were all talking about these things, the women mainly, till of my own accord I quietened down. I stood there, next to Tono and Ángelo and Milton. The four of us very still, not having to say anything because the women were doing all the talking.

The next day we went to look for the kid from the highlands, the one who looked after Don Vinicio Gutiérrez's beach house. There was no one staying in the beach house so only the kid was there, with his stupid face and cowardly eyes. You should have seen how he got when he saw us coming. I almost felt sorry for him. The kid was trembling, shaking all over. Couldn't even speak, till a couple of blows loosened his tongue. Then it all spilled out. Nothing we didn't already know. Told us they'd threatened him, he'd done it for his family, what little they gave him he sent back to the highlands, that they were struggling to make ends meet up there. The kid told us everything, showed us the phone they'd left him so he could keep them in the know. The gunmen would be here soon, he said, but he hadn't told them anything; only that the boss was coming to visit, which everyone already knew. We listened to him talk. He talked a long time, and after a while it was just gibberish, he was trying to buy himself time, none of it made any sense. He could already smell what was coming, that's for sure.

We threw him in the sea that same afternoon. A bunch of us from the town took a boat out, even Doña Ester came. The kid was tied up and wasn't talking anymore, he'd run out of words. Didn't even say anything when they lifted him up by the elbows: we threw him into the sea in silence, tied up tight, and he sank, all alone. Didn't even try to free himself: just went straight to the bottom. We threw the mobile phone in too, the same spot where the kid had gone down.

The gunmen arrived two days later. Some guys I know called to let me know they'd crossed the bridge. They left one guy stationed there, but the rest went on in a couple of 4x4s. They passed Don Vinicio Gutiérrez's beach house and stopped there a while, surely looking to get information out of the kid. People round there who'd been keeping an eye on things say they saw them get calmly out of the 4x4s, like they owned the place, but when they couldn't find the kid they started to look uneasy. They got out their weapons. Two of them went down to the beach for a while, walking back and forth until eventually they stopped and looked out at the sea. Like they knew. Somehow, they were starting to figure it out.

When they got to my hut we were ready for them. There were seven, plus the leader, and the lawyer wasn't with them. Course he wasn't: the lawyer was only needed for the paperwork, and papers meant nothing anymore. I was sitting on my chair in the hut with the rest of the guys, and outside were Milton, Ángelo and Tono. Almost all of them with rifles, me with my .22.

They got out of the two 4x4s with their weapons, grim-faced and serious. I heard them talking to Tono, heard his booming voice and one of the gunmen's sharp words. That was when I went out, me and all the others.

They weren't prepared for so many people, so many guns. They'd been on the alert after seeing Milton and Ángelo and Tono, but when they saw the rest of us come out of the hut they started to lose their nerve. They were old guns, some didn't even shoot straight, but they were still guns when it came down to it and all.

You're not welcome here, I stated.

Silence fell. A hard silence.

Your boss has already given up the land, their leader replied. He was wearing dark glasses and spoke strangely, like he wasn't talking to anyone in particular.

When land changes hands it gets registered in town, I told him. There's no record of any changes here.

The leader was still, calm.

And who do you believe this land belongs to?

Whoever the boss says it belongs to, I answered.

Bosses come and go, said the leader. Not you, though, you're always here.

Ubaldo's told you already, Tono said, taking a step forwards. A lot of blood's gonna get spilt over this land. And we've plenty of blood between us, enough to last a good long while.

Tono was being a bit dramatic, Andrés, I'm not gonna lie, but I still felt bolder, standing there with nothing but my .22, that little pistol that was like a toy next to the other weapons, but the click of the safety catch gave me confidence, with that click I felt calm, like the click marked a before and after, there in front of the hut.

The leader turned to look at his men and waited a moment, but in truth the game was already up. We won because we weren't worth the effort: it was that easy, Andrés, our blood wasn't worth them spilling theirs. The leader looked around him, turned to the sea, stood there a while. Then he started to walk back to his 4x4. They kept looking at us as they drove off, and we watched them heading back to the road.

What happened to them next I only heard second hand: on the way back they stopped before crossing the bridge to pick up the guy they'd posted there. But they couldn't find him. The gunman was gone, the people who live there had already taken him, and the more they looked the more men started coming out of their houses, weapons in hand, wearing a look that urged them on their way. In the end they decided just to go, didn't even ask about the guy they'd left on the bridge. They fired a couple of rounds into the sky before crossing and then continued on their way, knowing full well they were never going to get their guy back. The locals buried him right there, dug a hole somewhere in the mangroves and chucked the body in. God only knows how many bodies there are in those mangroves.

Ubaldo takes a sip of his beer and jiggles the can in his hand. Criminal not to finish it, really, he says, and downs the rest in one go. The empty aluminium can tinks as it touches the floor and Ubaldo adds that it's all over now, the gunmen know now that Monterrico won't give in so easily. Monterrico's more than they can handle, he says. Andrés gets himself another beer and opens one for Ubaldo.

They sit there for a long time drinking from their cans, their bodies still, nestled in their hammocks.

Ubaldo says a few things and so does Andrés, but not much can be heard over the breaking of the waves, over the water foaming as it recedes down the beach. From the sea all that's visible are two dark silhouettes framed by the thatched canopy, black shapes hanging from the ceiling. The wood creaks under the weight of the hammocks, and in the darkness of the night somebody asks:

Another beer?

TERRACE

We were on our way up the mountain in the jeep when Henrik said it was important to give women pleasure. The breeze coming in through the window had messed up his white hair, but his khaki outfit remained neat. Sure, you have to treat them with respect, he said, you have to be a gentleman, but you also have to give women pleasure. Henrik had been in a relationship with my mother for three years and we'd never talked about women, let alone about pleasure. In the passenger seat I opened the bottle of Coke and added a little more rum, trying not to spill any as we rattled along the dirt road. Without pleasure, the relationship's over, Henrik said. Pleasure's fundamental, otherwise it's dead in the water. He took the steering wheel in one hand and lifted his bottle to mine. Cheers.

But there are other things, too, right? Henrik turned to look at me. Apart from pleasure, I said. He smiled and crows' feet softened his gaze. Like what? I don't know, I said. Fidelity? Henrik laughed knowingly. If the rest of the relationship's going well, that'll come naturally.

The thing is, women are loyal, said Henrik. Your mum, for instance, there's no one more loyal than her. I leant forwards to peer at the top of the mountain, up where Henrik's land was. But with all that loyalty, you end up taking things for granted, Henrik continued. Time goes on and there you are, trusting nothing's going to change. Relationships are like plants, he said, gesturing outside, you have to nurture them. The road curved uphill and with the sun behind the mountains you could still see a few dry bushes. Plants need water, they need looking after. Some people even sing to them, he said, and shook his head, laughing. They sing to them!

I asked if he'd ever seen that. Seen what? People singing to their plants, I said. Henrik considered his response and I imagined, I'm not sure why, an older woman in the corner of a room, cooing a lullaby to the sad leaves of a potted plant. In all honesty, no, he said, I've never seen that. But people do it. Just because you haven't seen something doesn't mean it doesn't happen. That's what I'm getting at, he said. Sometimes it's the things you don't notice, those are the little things you need to look after in a relationship.

My wife, for example, may she rest in peace. He turned on the four-wheel drive – the road was steep and the tyres were starting to spew out dirt on either side. You know she was ill for a long time. I nodded. Twelve years, he said, twelve years she suffered. She helped me understand how important those little things are. Nothing compares to the way you look after someone when they're ill. Love, he said, true love, you only see it during illness. We drank from our plastic bottles and at the next turn Henrik rolled the window right down and flung his over the side of the mountain.

It sounds complicated, I said. The hardest part came after, he responded, the hard part is when you're alone. Night fell suddenly inside the jeep and Henrik turned on the headlights. I don't regret anything, he said, but there are always things left unfinished. You'd have to be made of stone not to think about that.

We kept climbing and the tops of the highest mountains started to appear, black silhouettes cut out against the opaque backdrop of the sky. Then I remembered the scar on Henrik's stomach, a little purple incision he'd tried to hide when we went to the beach. Henrik had donated a kidney to his wife and bore the mark of it somewhat shyly. I took a big swig from the bottle and said that not everyone would donate a kidney, that a sacrifice like that had to count for something.

That was no sacrifice, he said, donating a kidney to my wife was the greatest joy I could ever have had. An animal – a dog or a coyote – crossed the road in front of us and was lost in the undergrowth. Henrik kept talking: I was happy when I found out I could do the transplant. In those days I was even grateful for the horrible armchair where I slept in my wife's hospital room. Imagine what it's like to give the gift of a few years of life to the person you love most in the world. Can you imagine?

I wondered whether those years would be taken off his own life, off the life he shared with my mum. I filled up my bottle with what was left of the rum and gave it a shake to mix it. Good idea, he said, today is for celebrating, it's not every day you get to head up to a terrace in the mountains. Henrik had been building the terrace on his land bit by bit, using what little money he had left after paying off old debts. He'd been making trips of a day or two to take up planks of wood, a bag of cement, building the terrace over the course of a few weeks You'll see how nicely it's turning out, he said. He gestured towards the top of the mountain with his chin: it's a bit rough still, but as soon as it's ready we'll bring your mum.

We were almost there when he stopped the car by the side of the road, a rockface on one side and a cliff falling away on the other. We got out and he went to the boot to get another bottle of rum. He made up some fresh drinks and we stood there a while drinking by the cliff-edge. I've already put down some top soil by the terrace, he told me, for your mum's garden. She's crazy about her little plants, she'll love it up there. Henrik took a deep breath of country air. He filled our drinks again and closed the boot. He was quiet for a while, seeming to waver. It's not been easy, that terrace, he said. But it'll be OK, I know it, it'll be OK.

He went to stand at the edge of the cliff and began to pee. I got into the car and could hear the stream of urine still going, it seemed to go on forever. I heard him laugh. I needed that, he said from outside. When he got into the car he didn't put his seatbelt back on. That kidney'll last you a while yet, I said. Henrik turned to look at me. A while? he said. This kidney's gonna outlast us all. He laughed again. He looked happy. I was too. He started the jeep's engine and we went on up the mountain.

HENRIK

This one here's family, Henrik would say with a hand
on my shoulder, his fingers big and heavy but kind. The
other person would look at me, and look at him, and
then give a shy little smile before shaking my hand
and saying what a pleasure it was to meet one of
Henrik's relations. Later, when we all knew each other
better, Henrik would explain to whoever it was that he
was actually my stepdad, and might add more quietly, in
his deep Viking voice, that being a stepdad was almost
the same as being a dad, only to add in a different tone,
I've gotta be his pa or his step-pa, right, either that or
a paedo, and with that he'd laugh, and we'd laugh, even
though it was a strange thing to joke about and would
cause a certain amount of unease. But that was Henrik,
never one to worry about saying the right thing, not
because he wanted to be rude – he was actually prudent
by nature – but out of sheer desire to laugh and make
others laugh, even if that laughter would slip, so to speak,
in and out of the shadows of discomfort. The thing is,
Henrik didn't set much store by words (which are flimsy
and feeble, he'd say), but rather by that strange, invisible
energy that bodies emit, by the gestures and the honesty
that signal friendship, as he'd explain with a twinkle in
his eye, holding one of the cigarettes he'd offer round
when my mother wasn't there. But this would come
after the rum, of course, the rum and the conversation,
when Henrik had tuned in to his surroundings and was
navigating the fluid territory of drink.

They met one night by the lake, my mother and
Henrik, which wouldn't be important if the lake hadn't
somehow reflected their shared constancy, an unruffled,
uniform peace stretched over the surface, unchanging.
He'd lost his wife eight years earlier and his face still
bore the subtle marks of sleeplessness and dashes to
the hospital, as well as a certain proclivity to tears that
surprised my mother during their first encounter.

They were sitting in the rocking chairs set out by a
mutual friend in her little front garden. Out there, the
sounds and the heat and the silences of the party reached
them like messages from an indecipherable world. My
mother had lost her husband too, in her own way, and
if she visited her friend that weekend it was only because
she'd been sleepwalking ever since the separation, and
certain people had therefore taken her under their
wing, guiding her along the path of what they called
her convalescence.

I can picture my mother all wrapped up, her
little head poking out of blankets around her body.
She breathes deeply and watches the water from her
rocking chair. Henrik gazes at the lake too, towards
the lights on the opposite shore, but it's difficult to
know for certain whether he actually sees anything.
His eyes could just as well have lost their focus as he
thinks of something else, and if he's lost his focus it's
because he's found a memory, as he used to say after
being distracted. Time passes, and Henrik starts to
cry. He weeps, and keeps weeping, and my mother sits
in her seat, protected from the cold by her poncho,
those thick, coarse ponchos that her friend gets from
the villages down by the lakeside. Henrik weeps and
my mother is silent, and both bodies shake, but in
the darkness very little is visible and it doesn't really
matter.

I'd only just moved out when my mother called to invite me over for lunch. She wanted me to meet someone, she said, and the vagueness of her words made me think that some questionable individual had somehow found their way into our most intimate circle. I knew nothing about Henrik, about his immense hands or the involuntary twitch in his right cheek, a little tremble that would make him lower his gaze and pretend to concentrate on his food. A couple of references to his Scandinavian origins and certain facts about the sowing and harvesting of cardamom are all I remember from that conversation. But I also know that he bore the weight of the table well, so to speak, a round wooden table we'd had in the house for more than twenty years, one with stains and scars unknown to Henrik, hidden beneath the green tablecloth where his hand rested, palm open, holding my mother's little fingers. I was suspicious of his reserved manner, and spent a few minutes sizing him up from my seat, but had to give in to the candour of his silence.

He called me a few days later to ask if we could go for a drink. The Hotel Lux still had a bar made of dark wood, long and gleaming, but Henrik was waiting at one of the wobbly tables at the back. He squeezed my hand firmly and I could tell he was making an effort because of the muscles tensing in his face. He started talking slowly about nothing in particular, mentioning, among other things, his father, the only relative he kept in touch with, though their contact was sporadic, tenuous even. But you only get one father, he concluded rather sadly, breathing out slowly with his hands on the table. He wanted to talk to me, he said finally, to ask what I'd think if he were to move in with my mother. I have to ask, he said, for the sake of courtesy. I had to avoid his gaze, hiding for a moment behind a sip of rum and coke. My response was inadequate, maybe even unkind, but Henrik had the decency to raise his glass to family and the future, and we continued drinking, without a topic of conversation anymore but with no real need for one either.

I didn't know much about Henrik or the road to ruin he was treading. His easy laughter and contented look after Sunday lunches presaged a long, leisurely descent into old age. Domestic life suited him, he once told me, right before we left for a weekend trip my mother had organised, doubtless as an excuse for Henrik and I to get to know each other better. Henrik beamed the whole way there, gripping the steering wheel firmly with hands that were determined and capable of resolving any mishap. My mother watched him from her seat and smiled, moving her hand closer to his, the same smile she gave him later, when we were waiting in a roadside diner for our food to arrive, and Henrik introduced us to some stranger, a waiter or another customer he'd struck up conversation with, because it's a pleasure to have company, in this town of all places, Henrik said, especially with my family, next to this beautiful woman, on a night like this, under the light of the, well, maybe not the stars, but a lovely light nevertheless, now what do you mean you can't join us for a quick drink, you can't let a night like this pass you by.

The price of cardamom plummeted the year of that first lunch, bringing with it the shitstorm, as Henrik used to call it. His father, who had land up in the highlands and was over eighty, disappeared on one of his trips to the cardamom farm, La Corregidora. They called Henrik at three in the morning on a Tuesday to tell him they'd found him. Henrik explained to my mother, the phone still in his hand, that they'd just pulled his father down from the branch of a ceiba, where he'd been hanging for over twelve hours.

We all went together to the funeral. Some of his

father's colleagues barely looked at Henrik, as though seeing in his sadness the shame of his father's suicide. He calmly held my mother's hand while we waited in the cemetery for the priest to arrive. I suppose by then he already had other worries, new anxieties prompted by the letter that was found at the foot of the ceiba and the strange, sometimes incoherent sentences his father had written in it.

I started going round to the house more often. Henrik used to get home from work before my mother, and we'd sit on two little plastic chairs they kept in the garden. He'd make the drinks, using silver plated tongs to fish ice out of the little red bucket before letting it drop into the glass tumblers. It was there that the first fragments of that letter started to emerge, though I soon realised its words belonged to a correspondence much longer than those six handwritten pages. His talk went over my head, we both knew, and Henrik saved me the discomfort of listening to his explanations. He simply talked, mentioning details between sips, or after exhaling cigarette smoke, feeling his cheek with the tips of his fingers to assure himself everything was in order.

There are several fires that need putting out, he said. He spoke of vague, sometimes dark characters, contacts in the countryside, individuals who came and went from his story with no clear purpose, and he also spoke of La Corregidora, seized by the bank and taken over by the farmhands. Pretty vile what those boys have done, he murmured, hurt. He'd liquidated his father's assets. His salary from the export firm dwindled every month as the debts he'd inherited flooded in. Carlos, his friend and business partner, had agreed to lend him some money, which, naturally, had cooled their friendship. He had to pay the bank, the day labourers, his partner, and fatigue was beginning to show in his movements, his previously serene hands now conveying an air of dejection.

At his suggestion, we decided to start going out for our drinks. He'd call me when he finished work to arrange to meet in some bar in the city centre. His job at the export firm kept him out in the countryside, which gave him a certain freedom to look after his father's land. I noted with some concern how he'd draw those evenings out, prolonging our shared silence until there were no other punters left to hide it. My mother would be at home, awaiting Henrik's return, and we'd be in a bar, awaiting the return of God knows what.

He liked to hold his glass in both hands, on the table, turning it in his big, heavy, kind fingers. The men had money, he said on one of these occasions. We've got to keep that in mind, he continued, they've got money, there's not a lot of it around these days, but these men have definitely got it. They'd come to La Corregidora to visit him, he said, they arrived as soon as he got there, they were obviously well-informed because he never warned anyone when he was going to the farm. The boys had already started blocking him off at the entrance, the entrance to his own father's farm, he sighed, even though he was there specifically to talk to them, even though he wanted to reach an agreement with them so they could start to sort this whole mess out. In short, he said, they came to see me, these men, very friendly, very polite, gentlemen really, treated me very respectfully. Don Henrik, they said, you're letting this land go to waste, it's bleeding dry as we speak. Can't you see the seedlings are all withered, look at your wretched little cardamom plants, why don't you let us help you out, if you don't this whole place is going to the dogs, Don Henrik, just look at the boys, or worse, look at the bank, they're not going to do you any favours. You know we're here, Don Henrik, we'll happily take the farm off your hands, you know that these problems with the bank, with the boys, there's a way of fixing them all.

I'd see my mother in the afternoons sometimes, when I went round to the house for a coffee, but we always tried to avoid the subject. She knew Henrik and I were meeting up and viewed those evenings with a distant but benign curiosity. I ran into him there once, when I was waiting in the living room for my mother to get off the phone. I was examining the five or six dolls – creatures with disturbing faces – that had appeared on the shelf on the wall when I felt him approach. After exchanging a few words we looked at the dolls together in silence. Trolls, said Henrik eventually, they bring good luck. They had noses shaped like turnips and opaque, almost malicious gazes. He raised his finger slowly and drew a circle round the figures. That's what they say in Norway, that trolls look after the house. He was going to say something else but seemed to change his mind. After a while he said goodbye, suggesting we meet up soon, before glancing one last time at the line of little dolls.

I'm glad that you're spending time together, my mother said that afternoon, especially now Henrik's started walking with his shoulders hunched, like something's pressing him down towards the ground. She was much better informed than I was, knew his movements and silences, knew details from the letter that I did not. That's what Henrik had told me, that there were things in the letter that couldn't be explained, things that couldn't be spoken of, except to my mother, of course, from whom nothing should be kept.

She realised that Henrik was on the edge of an abyss, could see the shame brought on by every trip to the bank, every return from the farm. Things were not improving. She told me, as we drank our coffee, that his partner was suing him for missing his loan repayments. You're only supposed to sue your enemies, she said. It hit him hard, she went on. He didn't understand how someone could play him like that after a loan given in friendship. Talk about kicking a man when he's down, said my mother, and then fell silent. But at least, she continued, looking into the bottom of her cup, in moments like these, the wolves take off their sheep's clothing.

★

We're here to celebrate, Henrik said when he saw me. The bar in Hotel Lux was empty at that time of the afternoon, but Henrik already had a bottle of rum on the table, unusual for him because he always drank by the glass, ordering them one at a time, gesturing to the bar so the waiter would come over and talk to him a while, because Henrik hadn't lost his love of casual conversation, even if it was limited to passing the time of day. But now he had the bottle on the table, two glasses, a little metal ice bucket, and slices of lime that he squeezed into my drink before gesturing to a seat and asking me to sit down, because that night we had cause for celebration. His face was shiny and his cheek was twitching intensely, as though he'd given free rein to his tic. Today things changed, he said as he held up his glass for a toast. The men and I reached an agreement, he said, they accepted the offer, so now it's just a matter of signing the deeds, and meeting with a notary. But they'll sort that out, the notary. You just look after the deeds, Don Henrik, they said, so all I have to do is bring the deeds, and a pen so I can sign them. He took a long drink from his glass. Sign them and then, obviously, hand over the farm.

That night we drank until late. Henrik's initial talkativeness receded with every drink, his words blurring with the alcohol and the murmur of a few other customers in the bar. At some point silence arrived, reliable as ever, taking a seat at our table with all the calm in the world. After a while Henrik began to play with a slice of lime, lifting it and observing it closely before smashing it with his thumb against the table's wooden surface. He annihilated half a lime that way. He picked up the last slice and held it against the light coming from the bar.

They're no farmers, he said eventually. Those men, they're no farmers, all they've got is the moustache. He gave the ghost of a smile, as bitter as any I'd seen, and brought the little slice of lime to his lips. But what was he supposed to do, he asked, if the bank had cut him off and the boys were in for the long haul. He sucked on the lime and wiped his mouth with the back of his hand before meeting my eyes. You understand what I'm saying, don't you? Tell me, he repeated, louder this time, do you understand what I'm saying? One of the waiters turned to look in our direction. I wanted to answer, even though deep down I didn't really want to understand, and if I understood anything between the rum and that silence it was that I didn't have any answers. There'll always be family, I murmured after a while, conscious that these were vague words, and felt myself blush, the heat of the drink mixing with a different heat rising up my neck. Henrik watched me, almost curiously, and then nodded, raising his glass to clink it against mine. Of course, he said, there'll always be family.

By the time I made it out into the street there were barely any lights left on. He'd stay a while, he said, he wanted to sweat it out a bit longer. He went over to the bar, his steps surer than my own, and let himself drop onto one of the stools. All the other customers had gone, but Henrik's loyalty to the Lux was rewarded with the privilege of one last drink at his discretion. We parted with a handshake and when I got outside I had to lean against a wall, letting the concrete take the weight of my body. A halogen sign lit up the opposite street corner: dust particles were floating nervily in the pale light. I walked towards them, and got a shock when I looked down. My hands were white, transparent, almost alien in the phosphorescent dust quivering around me. I hid them hurriedly in my pockets, making sure no one else had seen what I'd just seen, and set off down the street to the guesthouse where I lived.

When I woke up the next morning I was in a bad way and I didn't go out except to buy something to eat. I spent almost the entire weekend in bed, and by Sunday night knew I wouldn't talk to Henrik that week, not to him nor my mother, that it would be better to give him some time, give them some time, and something about that certainty made me wrap up warmer during those days, eat more heartily, prepare myself for things I thought I could sense but didn't know for sure. The call came on Monday.

It's Henrik, said the voice. He coughed a little and I said hello. Your mother's somewhat indisposed, he said, she's had a bit of a fright, nothing serious, but you know what it's like when you've had a shock. He waited a moment, as though expecting me to agree, but in truth I didn't know what kind of shock he was talking about. I asked him. He ignored me. You'll have heard that I didn't sell the farm, he said. It didn't seem like the right thing to do, he added, and then repeated the words more deliberately: the right thing, I didn't think it was the right thing. In short, he said, there have been a few difficulties, and it would be good if you could come by the house. It would be better to talk at home, he repeated, better at home than like this.

It was Henrik who opened the door. He leant out to glance over my shoulder before shaking my hand and letting me in. Then he led me into the living room where we waited. She's on her way, was all he said, and shortly after my mother emerged from her room and came over to hug me. She sat down next to Henrik on the sofa and looked out of the big window on the other side of the living room. In the garden, the wind began to shift the black leaves of the plants. Better if you explain, she said to Henrik. He took her hand, which seemed to disappear inside his big, kind fingers. From the rocking chair where I sat, my mother looked fragile but calm.

Well, what can I say, said Henrik, except that the men were rather put out. You know how touchy these people can be, he added, turning to my mother, nothing new about that. I told you before, he went on, looking at me now, that they were real gentlemen when they talked to me at the farm, very polite the whole time. And in exchange for all that politeness, well, they think they're owed something in return. I looked over Henrik's shoulder at the shelf where the trolls were waiting in a line. That's how they see it, anyway, he added, otherwise the phone call would have gone differently.

They were very rude, my mother then said. I was surprised by her tone because she sounded hurt, as though she'd been insulted by a close friend. Henrik took her hand in both of his and began stroking it. They treated her very badly, he said. They asked for me, and she asked them who was calling. I asked what they wanted, my mother chimed in. She shifted her body closer to Henrik's. They insulted me, said a whole load of nasty things, and then they hung up.

The second call was different, she continued in a quieter voice. It was a couple of hours after the first one and I answered thinking it would be Henrik, because he was on his way back from the highlands and had said he'd call. The phone rings and I pick up and they start talking straight away, without asking a thing. The voice says first things first, I need to stop being scared, because if I'm scared, if I start shaking and stop thinking clearly then I won't understand anything, and then yes, I'll have good reason to be scared. But that's just the worst case scenario. The voice asks me to listen. I listen. It says there are certain kinds of agreements that can't just be forgotten. Because that's how they prefer to interpret what's happened, says the voice, as a slip of the mind, and they don't even want to contemplate the idea that the agreement has been broken, because an agreement is, after all, a question of honour, a pact between gentlemen, an understanding, and what's left if we can't even understand each other. Fear, says the voice. That's what's left. Because we've been very generous, and Henrik knows that, the voice adds, Henrik knows how generous we've been, and to reject that generosity, to renege on that agreement, could lead to one thing only. We all know what that one thing is.

That was two days ago, Henrik says now. Two days ago we received those two calls, but the important thing is to stay calm. Your mum knows I always keep a .22 in the car. We've got it in the house now. We have to stay calm, he says, and protect ourselves: we'll only use the .22 in an emergency. Above all we have to protect the house and that's why I'm here, it's better that I stay in the city for a few days, because I'm not going to leave your mum here by herself.

And besides, continues Henrik, today when I went to the front door the neighbour told me there'd been a man hanging around, that a man stopped on the other side of the street and stood there, smoking, leaning against the railing, and he was there for ages according to the neighbour, smoking and watching the house. He had a very odd habit, the neighbour told me, a way of smoking that first surprised and then annoyed him, because he only took one drag of each cigarette, this guy would light a cigarette and take one drag before flinging it down onto the pavement like he didn't want a used cigarette anywhere near him, the neighbour said, and he got through cigarette after cigarette like that, taking his time between each one, but keeping to his method, watching the house, taking one drag per cigarette, until he left.

Henrik stands up from the sofa and lights a cigarette. I'll be right back, he says going into the kitchen. He returns with glasses and ice. He puts them on the little coffee table and lifts the bottle, touching it to the lip of each glass to pour out a generous glug of amber rum, and then goes round the table, a glass for my mother, another for me, a third for him, before he sits down again, cigarette in one hand and rum in the other, and says something about life and its twists and turns and its cartwheels, mainly its cartwheels, the cartwheels are when everything goes to shit, he says, and then he is very still, the smoke from his cigarette rising silkily from between his fingers.

They get up when the drinks are finished. We need to rest, says my mother, rest and consider our options, she adds, looking at him. They walk together to their room. They go hand in hand, taking little steps, but there's something in the way they move, a shared equilibrium that reconciles my mother's small figure with Henrik's all-encompassing presence. Before crossing the threshold my mother turns and tells me it's late, that it's dangerous to be out in the street, that it would be better if I stayed over. I say goodnight before pouring myself another drink, and then move to the sofa. The burn of the rum and the soft cushion at my back give me a pleasant sense of wellbeing. I must be on my third drink when I fall asleep.

A thick, sack-like fabric wraps my body and head and I wake up terrified, suffocating. It's Henrik who's covering me, I realise, with one of the ponchos from down by the lake. I keep my eyes shut, paralysed by sweat and shock. I feel the rum on his breath as he stretches the cover out over me, tucking in my feet. Something wooden creaks and I crack my eyes open for a second to see that Henrik has sat down in the rocking chair, drink in hand.

When I wake up again it's cold and the first thing I see is the poncho on the floor. I try to cover myself, pulling it onto the sofa, and notice Henrik standing on the other side of the living room. He's leaning to one side, his face against the glass of the big window looking out onto the garden, and he's holding the curtain open lightly with the tips of his fingers. He glances at me and lifts a finger to his lips. He's wearing a white dressing gown and on his feet are thin socks pulled up over his ankles. He brings his head to the glass again, and it's a second before I understand that the thing in his other hand is the .22.

The outside light is on, dimly filtering through the green of the garden plants. Further back the dark silhouettes of bushes are swaying in the breeze. Henrik starts to move away from the window, still facing the garden, his back to the wall as he moves round the living room. His steps are uncertain, faltering, and he has to steady himself on the shelf, swiping at the trolls as he goes past. One of them falls to the floor and I hear Henrik breathing heavily as he kneels and then gets down on all fours to look for the doll, before eventually standing up and returning it to its place.

Finally he reaches for the garden door and opens it with his left hand. He waits a moment before taking a tentative step outside. His white dressing gown glows bright in the darkness. He takes another step. I sit up on the sofa and see the pistol in his hand, grasped firmly against his hip. He is still, his head bent forwards. He's examining the bushes at the bottom of the garden. I guess he can't see much because he stays like that for a few long seconds, the weapon still, trying to keep his balance. I sense that there's someone else in the living room and when I turn around my mother's there, pale, wrapped in a blanket. Easy now, she says. Henrik points the pistol at the plants, his hand shaking, and I start to get up too. Easy now, my mother says again. She puts her hand on my shoulder, holding me back. Wait here, she says, wait here. She sits down next to me and both of us are still. Henrik shakes his head, and we hear a murmur from outside. It's Henrik, without a doubt, but his words, or sounds that might be words, come from somewhere very different. We're silent, my mother and I, watching the window, watching his body tremble. Henrik turns towards us, looking back inside, tears streaming down his face, and raises the gun to the sky. Then the shots begin.

CHARCO PRESS

Director & Editor: Carolina Orloff
Director: Samuel McDowell

www.charcopress.com

Trout, Belly Up was published on
90gsm Munken Premium Cream paper.

The text was designed using Bembo 11.5 and ITC Galliard.

Printed in October 2020 by TJ Books
Padstow, Cornwall, PL28 8RW using responsibly sourced paper
and environmentally-friendly adhesive.